I HID MY VOICE

I HID MY VOICE

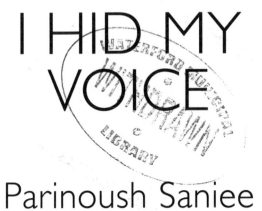

Parinoush Saniee

Translated by Sanam Kalantari

Little, Brown

LITTLE, BROWN

First published in Great Britain in 2016 by Little, Brown

Copyright © Parinoush Saniee 2016
Translation copyright © Sanam Kalantari 2016

The moral right of the author has been asserted.

A CIP catalogue record for this book
is available from the British Library.

ISBN 978-1-4087-0752-4

Typeset in Goudy by M Rules
Printed and bound in Great Britain by
Clays Ltd, St Ives plc

Papers used by Little, Brown are from well-managed forests
and other responsible sources.

MIX
Paper from
responsible sources
FSC
www.fsc.org   FSC® C104740

Little, Brown
An imprint of
Little, Brown Book Group
Carmelite House
50 Victoria Embankment
London EC4Y 0DZ

An Hachette UK Company
www.hachette.co.uk

www.littlebrown.co.uk

For my dearest Niloofar and Kamyar

I HID MY VOICE

CHAPTER 1

'Shahaab, is this you?'

'Yeah.'

'You were so small! Who's this hugging you so tightly?'

I stared at the picture. Who was it? Could it really be . . . ?

My heart sank and my tongue felt heavy. I looked around bewildered, searching for a way out. The house was crowded. Half the guests had already arrived. Where had my mother found all these people? Was growing up really such a big deal? With this party they were trying to remind me that I was twenty years old now, practically a man, but I didn't feel a great change in myself. They were all talking, laughing and moving through the house. I wasn't sure how to behave as a host. A few more arrived and the others gathered around them. I took advantage of this opportunity and ran up the stairs. Despite the short flight I began to pant as I went up and opened the door at the top.

A familiar voice inside me said: 'What the hell is wrong with you now?' And, as always, my knee-jerk reaction was: 'I don't know . . .'

I could still hear them downstairs. This wasn't the calm and quiet I was looking for. I walked out on to the terrace, shutting the door behind me. I felt a cool breeze against my hot forehead and took a deep breath. I looked at the forbidden steps leading

1

from the terrace to the rooftop and felt a jolt of pain in my back. Every time I saw them something would happen in my confused mind, and I would feel this pain. I climbed the steps. How long had it been since I'd last been up here? A day? A hundred years? The past came rushing in and I was moving backwards at break-neck speed. I felt like I was growing smaller and smaller. As I sat down in the middle of the roof, I was once again a four- or five-year-old boy, mute and terrified.

I became sensitive to the word 'dumb' from the day I realized I actually *was* dumb. Whenever they called me that I would feel angry, scream, break things or have a go at someone and cause trouble. But that all changed as soon as I accepted the truth. I no longer grew angry every time I heard it. Instead, it was as if something was stuck in my throat or as if someone was clawing at my heart. All the colours around me grew dim and the sun stopped shining. I would crawl into a corner, place my head on my folded knees and try to make myself as tiny as possible. So tiny that no one would notice me again. I didn't want to play any more and I would forget how to laugh. Nothing made me happy. Those hours would sometimes stretch to a day or two. Do you realize how long that is for a four-year-old? Maybe as long as a couple of months are for an adult. I think it was better when I reacted violently. They would tell me off and hit me, and I would cry, but everything would be over quicker. It would never take more than an hour or two.

At first, before I knew what it meant, I thought being dumb was a good thing. When they called me that it made me happy because they all said it so joyfully. My cousin Khosrow was the first person to realize that I was dumb and he was the one who gave me the name. As soon as he saw me he'd say, 'What a nice dumb boy! Come and do a headstand, and I'll give you some sweets. Good boy!'

I would do whatever he wanted and he would laugh, cheer me on and give me a prize. My other cousin Fereshteh also liked me very much. 'My little dumbo!' she would call me and give me a hug. I loved her smell. She would laugh at the things I did, and buy me sweets and ice cream. I liked those things but, honestly, what I liked more was making her happy. I was willing to do anything just to make her happy. They always laughed when they called me 'dumb' so I assumed it was a nice word. I didn't realize that when people laughed it didn't necessarily mean they were happy. After all, I was dumb.

The days seemed brighter before I discovered these dark truths. The sky was clearer. I could spend hours in our small garden examining the earth, the leaves, and the brown worms that came out after the rain. I found something new every minute. Our lone tree was a sympathetic friend that would blossom every time we returned from our New Year trip. I knew it did this from the joy of seeing us again. A few days later its blossoms would fall and it would look different. And later it would produce delicious red cherries. Producing cherries was its responsibility, but the only reason for its blossoms was to welcome me back home, since I loved it more than anyone else.

Sometimes I would play with the light shining through the folds of a curtain, absorbed in the flecks of dust floating in the air.

At night the stars shone brightly, but the moon, the moon was something else. Just like a headstrong child, it didn't follow any rules. Its job was to light up the night sky, but it wouldn't show up if it didn't feel like it. Instead, it would suddenly appear at unexpected times, creeping up to the middle of the sky. Some mornings I would see it next to the sun. Smiling mischievously, it would turn pale so no one would notice it. It was always playful, too, chasing me around the pool and stopping without fail at the exact moment I did. It never took an extra step by mistake. I came to believe that an invisible strand tied us together; that it only followed me because it was my friend. I would lie on the bed in the garden and look at it. Everyone else moved around, but the moon didn't follow them. It was just like me. No one could force it to do something it didn't want to. Yes, I was the moon, and Arash was the sun, always on time and never doing anything wrong.

3

In those days before realizing my dumbness, I was at the peak of consciousness. My soul was never again as aware as it was back then.

I realized I was mute one terrible day. I was headed to my uncle's house, which was a few houses down from ours. Khosrow was playing with his friends on the street. He wasn't like Arash, who was always reading a book. Instead he was playful and mischievous. My uncle always told him, 'Look at Arash! He's in your class even though he's a year younger. He comes top every year, while you fail and have to retake your exams. He's going to become a doctor and you'll end up as his chauffeur. Just mark my words!'

Fataneh, Khosrow's mother, got annoyed every time she heard this. 'Rubbish! My son can fit ten like him in one pocket.' I would look at Khosrow's pocket but it seemed too small to fit anyone inside. 'Plus Arash isn't younger by a whole year; it's just a few months. They sent their son to school early, while my son is in the exact class he should be. The way you say they're in the same year even though he's older makes it sound like he's missed a year!'

'Read my lips. One of these years he will!'

'*Pffft!* If he doesn't make it to the top it will be because of you. They praise their children while you're constantly putting down our poor son.'

Fataneh, my uncle's wife, was weird. Whenever my mum wasn't around she would say, 'That bitch thinks it's a big deal she went to university. As if every loser who goes to university needs to show off. I'll let her have it the next time I see her. Thank goodness this one is an imbecile, otherwise she would be bragging about her kids non-stop.'

She would say these things in front of me, and since I was mute and didn't speak, she was sure I wouldn't report it to Mother. But she would forget everything she'd said as soon as she saw her. Instead of 'letting her have it', she would sweet-talk her and say, 'You're educated so you understand things better than we do.'

Mother would get embarrassed and reply, 'That's not true!' I felt sorry for Fataneh since she forgot everything so fast. If I could have talked, I would have helped remind her.

On that fateful day, Khosrow called as soon as he saw me, 'Hey there, Shahaab, you dummy, come over here.' I ran over and stood next to him. He knelt in front of me, placed his hands on my shoulders and said, 'Good boy. I want you to show my friends what a nice dumb boy you are, and I'll buy you a huge ice cream afterwards. Put your head down here and lean your legs against the wall.'

The ground was dirty and I didn't like dirt. I looked around for a better place to put my head. Khosrow said, 'What are you waiting for? You used to be a nice dummy. Hurry up and put your head down for me.'

I had to do what he wanted. I happily placed my head on the ground and my legs against the wall. Everyone started to laugh. Then he said, 'Now roll around so you get dusty all over.'

Mum told me off whenever I got my clothes dirty.

'Hurry up and be a good boy. Come and cheer him.' They all began to clap. I had no choice; everyone wanted me to do it, so I lay down on the ground.

The kids clapped harder and said, 'Good job, dummy! Roll around, roll around!'

The more I rolled around the happier they got. I knew that Mum would scold me but it wasn't important, the happiness of Khosrow and his friends was worth it.

Faraj the fatty said, 'Will you do anything he asks you?'

'Of course he will. He's my very own dummy.'

Faraj looked around and said, 'Then tell him to drink from this ditch.'

Farhad replied, 'He won't do it. No matter how dumb he is. He's not going to drink that.'

Faraj said, 'But Khosrow says he'll do whatever he asks him to.'

Khosrow bragged, 'Yes! He'll do anything I want.'

'I'll bet he won't drink from the ditch. What do you say? Willing to bet?'

5

'What are you offering?'

'My pen knife. But if he doesn't drink it you have to give me your bike.'

'What are you talking about? A bike for a knife! I'm not the idiot here, he is.'

'Okay, then let me have it for a week.'

'No. Just one day.'

'Fine, it's a deal.'

Khosrow walked towards me and placed his arm around my shoulder again and said, 'Shahaab, I want you to show these kids that you're a good boy. Come and drink a bit from this ditch, and I'll take you to the cafe and buy you a big sandwich and some ice cream afterwards. Okay?'

No! I didn't want to do it. Ugh! The water in the ditch was black and had worms in it. It smelled disgusting. I turned around.

'Listen, Shahaab. Don't make me look bad in front of my friends. Don't you love me? Just one sip.'

Farhad said, 'He won't do it. Like I said, it doesn't matter how dumb he is, he still understands he shouldn't drink it.'

'Yes, he will. If I ask him, he'll do it. Won't you? Come on, don't be a sissy, just one sip.'

I was afraid of the worms in the water. I pulled out my hand from his grip and ran towards the house. I hadn't taken more than a couple of steps when he grabbed my shirt from behind.

'Hey, where do you think you're going? You're not going anywhere until you take a sip from this ditch.'

I wanted to cry and felt sick. He pushed on my neck, moving my head closer to the ditch.

'Come on, kids, cheer him on. See, he's going to drink it.'

No one clapped. It looked like they were all about to be sick. He pushed my head into the ditch. The tip of my nose touched the smelly slime. It felt like I was choking.

Suddenly a miracle occurred. His hand went limp and I was able to pull my head away. I could hear Arash yelling, 'Let him go, stupid!' I fell to the side. I hadn't drunk any water but I had slime on my face. I threw up right there.

6

'What do you want with this kid, you idiot! Are you insane? He'll die if he drinks this water.'

'Your brother is the idiot! He's willing to do anything for an ice cream. He was going to drink this water just for a sandwich. Isn't that right?'

Faraj said, 'He's right. Your brother is crazy. You shouldn't let him out.'

'Shut up. You're crazy yourself.'

'You're both crazy. If you weren't crazy you wouldn't study so much.'

Arash grabbed my hand angrily and pulled me home.

CHAPTER 2

I was feeding Shadi. I heard the door slam but didn't pay any attention until I saw Shahaab covered in mud and slime, holding Arash's hand. I screamed, 'Oh my God! What happened to you? Didn't I tell you not to get your clothes dirty?'

Arash, angry and on the verge of tears, told me the whole story. I could feel the blood rushing to my head with every word. I was shaking all over. I picked Shadi up, grabbed Shahaab's hand, and without any attention to what I was wearing, walked towards Hossein and Fataneh's house. I let go of Shahaab's hand once we got there and pressed the door-bell until they opened the door. As soon as it opened, I pulled Shahaab's hand again, crossed the garden, walked into the hall and came face to face with Fataneh, who was rushing towards me, worried. Hossein, Shahin, Fereshteh and Khosrow were in front of the TV. There was a tea-tray on the coffee table. Fereshteh ran forwards and took Shadi from my arms. I took no heed of her. It was as if I couldn't see anyone except for Khosrow. My heart was beating fast and with a voice that sounded unfamiliar to my own ears, I yelled, 'What do you want with this child? Is he the only one you can bully? Didn't you think he would be sick if he drank that water? Why do you pick on him so much?'

Khosrow answered innocently, 'It's not my fault. He's willing to do anything for ice cream and sweets. The kids tease him because he's dumb. I watch out for him so he doesn't get beaten up.'

'What do you mean "dumb"? Aren't you ashamed of yourself, calling him names? He isn't dumb at all.'

Hossein calmly said, 'Don't upset yourself. Why are you so angry? Some kids are less intelligent than others. Some like Arash are talented and have a high IQ, and others like this one are a bit slow.'

'He's not slow at all. You're all labelling him.'

Fataneh said derisively, 'Why don't you want to accept the truth? A child who hasn't talked by this age must be retarded.'

'His lack of speech has nothing to do with being retarded. His doctor says that some kids start talking later. It has nothing to do with his intelligence.'

'Rubbish! We've never seen a smart, intelligent four-year-old who doesn't talk. My Khosrow began talking when he was still crawling.'

I answered with exasperation, 'No, he started talking when he was still in your belly, but as you can see, he isn't smart at all! So talking early or late has nothing to do with being smart.'

Fataneh pursed her lips and said, 'What did you say? Hossein, did you hear what she said about my son?'

Hossein got up and walked towards me, and trying to remain calm said, 'Try to control yourself. Instead of getting angry you should seriously think of doing something about this child.'

My voice kept getting louder and louder, 'There's nothing wrong with him. You should seriously think of doing something about your own child.'

Shahin said, 'Maryam, that's not nice. My brother didn't say anything hurtful. He's just worried about your son and thinks you should take him to a doctor. All the children in our family are clever. This sort of case is very uncommon.'

'All the children in my family are clever too. Don't worry about this one either. There's nothing wrong with him.'

I took Shadi from Fereshteh's arms and turned to Shahaab who was looking at me startled.

'The next time someone calls you "dumb", smack him in the mouth. Do you understand?'

I couldn't stand being there any more, so grabbing Shahaab's hand I turned and went home without saying goodbye.

I knew that my reaction would seem very strange to my husband's family, who before this had always seen me as a quiet, shy person. The whole situation would probably explode with all kinds of repercussions.

As soon as I got home my anger subsided into feelings of despondency and fatigue. I was out of words, as though I'd said all there was to say. I gave Shahaab a bath and put fresh clothes on him. He never took his eyes off me. I couldn't tell anything from his eyes. I knew that he was surprised by my unusual reaction, but I wasn't sure what he thought of it. My calm exterior belied my inner agitation.

My anger was rekindled when Nasser got home. I complained to him about the insults they had aimed at our child. And as always, he looked at me in silence and chewed on his moustache.

'What do you want me to do? Maybe they're right.'

I looked at him for a few seconds, and then jumped up and yelled, 'Do *you* think this child is retarded too?'

'If he isn't retarded, why won't he talk? Didn't the doctor say there was nothing wrong with his hearing or the rest of his body? Maybe he has a mental problem.'

'Stop this nonsense! There's nothing wrong with my child. I know it. He talks to me with his eyes.'

'You're a mother. You don't want to accept the truth.'

Arash took his father's side, 'He's right, Mum! If he wasn't dumb he wouldn't do whatever they asked him.'

'He's a child. He doesn't understand right from wrong. You're his older brother. You have to look out for him.'

'It's none of my business. I'm ashamed of walking around with him. Everyone says, "Your brother's an idiot." I don't want a brother like him.'

'Shut up! Instead of keeping other people from saying such things, you're repeating them yourself?'

'Maryam, he's right. Try to accept the truth.'

'Leave me alone. My child is not an idiot. To hell with you!'

And I began to cry out loud.

CHAPTER 3

I was sitting in a corner, carefully following every word as Mother, in both anger and sorrow, described the incident to Father. My hatred grew every second, and I was curious to see my father's reaction. I was hoping he would go and take revenge on them all, to finish what Mother had started and teach my uncle's family a lesson. But instead he calmly stood there and said they were right.

Enraged from seeing Mother's tears and hearing the words spoken by Father and Arash, I had to do something. I noticed the invitingly open door to Arash's room. I quietly crept inside. I knew I wasn't allowed to touch his things. This had been made clear to me ever since I could remember. The lamp on his desk was on. His books and papers were scattered all over, and his new fountain pen was next to the large sheet of card that had taken up two days of his time. I picked up the bottle of black ink that came with the pen. I could hear Arash saying, 'I'm ashamed of walking around with him. Everyone says, "Your brother's an idiot."' I carefully poured the ink over the card and all his books and papers. I grew calm as soon as I dropped the empty bottle on the floor. It was as if the fire inside me had died down. I quietly walked out of the room and went up the stairs.

Hearing Arash screaming, my parents ran into his room. I stuck my head out of the door in order to listen to them better. Arash was sobbing. 'He's ruined my poster. I was supposed to hand it in tomorrow. What am I going to tell the teacher now? I worked so hard.'

Father asked, 'How did the ink tip over?'

'It didn't tip over by itself. Shahaab must have done it.'

Mother said, 'Nonsense! Shahaab has never touched anything in your room before. Are you calling him a vandal too? The wind probably tipped the bottle.'

'Your mother's right. I don't think Shahaab would do such a thing. It's never happened before. Although there's no wind here and the windows are shut!'

This was the first time I had ruined something. Revenge tasted sweet. I was a bit scared, but when it was all over I calmly lay on the big squeaky bed that I'd recently inherited from Arash. It didn't matter any more how much I hated this bed and preferred my own cosy cot that they had given to Shadi. Or how much I wanted a new bed with drawers, just like the one they had bought for Arash. I didn't even get jealous when Shadi played up like every other night, and went and slept in Mother's bed.

I pretended to be asleep when Mother came in to remind me to change into pyjamas and brush my teeth. Surprised, she turned off the lights and went out again. Even darkness didn't scare me any longer. It was as if that day's experiences had made me grow up. I'm not sure but I think it was that same night that I discovered Asi and Babi, who were always hiding in a corner. I described the bitter events of the day for them. They comforted me and praised me for what I'd done.

Asi said, 'You did the right thing. He deserved it.'

Babi kissed me, and the three of us laughed under the blankets.

Asi continued, 'Tomorrow we'll deal with his father. He called us retarded too.' We thought about different things we could do to the things he loved most.

13

Finally, with some fear and trepidation, Babi said, 'His car—'
That night I fell asleep later than ever.

I woke up next morning at the sound of Father's car. I ran to
the window.

Asi said, 'Too bad. We're late.' But Babi was happy and took a
deep breath. My heart beat fast the entire day and I got butterflies in my stomach remembering the evening's plans.

Mother asked several times, 'What's wrong with you today?
Why do you keep staring off into space?'

I went into the garden when Father arrived. I couldn't give
up on taking revenge. It was as if my life depended on it. A cool
breeze made me shiver. It was dark outside. Under the light from
a bedroom window I found Mother's pruning shears. It was a large
pair of shears that I was scared of and wasn't allowed to touch. I
calmly walked towards the car and sat down. I tried to force the
shears into one of the tyres but they wouldn't go in.

Asi said, 'The front tyre may be softer.' I tried that one too but
it didn't work.

Babi said, 'That's enough. Let's go.'

Asi said, 'No! Draw something on the car.' I drew some lines
with the tip of the shears.

Babi sang, 'Eyes and eyebrows, now a nose, a mouth and a
circle for the face, a stick, a stick, and now the belly ...'* The
lights in the garden suddenly went on.

My mother looked surprised. 'Is that you, Shahaab? What are
you doing outside? Come in, you'll catch a cold.'

I was so startled that I dropped the shears with a loud thud.

Father's face appeared behind Mother, and he yelled angrily,
'What was that? What are you up to, you scoundrel?' He put on
his slippers and ran outside and grabbed my hand. I was shaking.
My mouth was as dry as bark. Mother ran after Father, who had
picked up the shears and was looking at the lines on his car. I
looked up at his face, which had gone dark. I knew he loved his
car, but hadn't realized how much. He lifted his hand.

* A Persian rhyme used by children to draw a stick figure.

14

Mother threw herself forwards and pulled me out of his grip. 'What are you doing? Be careful! You're holding the shears. You'll hurt him.' She took them away from him.

'Do you see this? Do you see? Go on and say he's not mad!'

I hadn't noticed Arash, but he said, 'See! He *must* have poured the ink on my poster last night.'

'Something must have happened. He wouldn't do such a thing for no reason. You must have said something to hurt him.'

'What are you talking about? I've just got here and haven't seen him all day.'

Arash sobbed, 'What did I do to him yesterday to deserve what he did? I even got into an argument for him. If he'd drunk that slimy water he'd be dead by now. And instead of thanking me he ruined all my hard work.'

I wanted to laugh. Arash was such an idiot. That was before we got home and he said he was ashamed of me. That's why I poured the ink. I guess he didn't understand the difference between before and after.

Father kept rubbing his hand over the scratches on his car and was growing crosser by the minute. He came towards me as I was trying to hide behind Mother, grabbed my arm and with a voice that shook with fury said, 'I'll teach you a lesson not to do such things again.' With his large hands he slapped the back of my head and my neck. I was so scared that I didn't feel any pain.

'Stop hitting him! He can't help it. He must have had a reason.'

'What reason? The only reason is that he's abnormal. I'll lock him in his room. He's not allowed any supper either. And stop interfering. You've spoiled him enough already.'

I sat on my bed. Asi and Babi were quiet. I listened to the voices downstairs. I could hear all four of them. First they talked about my being mute and then Shadi said something with her baby voice that made Father laugh. They had supper together. Arash talked about school. Good for them. They were a real family. I was forgotten. I felt abandoned and realized I wasn't one of them.

15

My heart felt heavy. I said to Asi, 'They don't love me. I am not their child.'

Babi who couldn't stand being sad for long said, 'Mother loves you. She buys you stuff and feeds you, and sometimes kisses you. If she hadn't been there tonight he would have killed you with those shears.'

'I know, but the rest of them don't love me. Especially Father and Arash. I don't love them either. I'll show them, just wait and see.'

That night after they all went to bed, Mother brought me a small sandwich. She sat on the bed next to me, looked at me with worried eyes and said, 'What's got into you? You never used to do such things.'

I stuck my head under the blanket. Why didn't she understand that I *had* to do these things?

I completely changed from that night on. Every laugh seemed to make fun of me and I was always searching for ways to take revenge, especially on Khosrow and my uncle's family. But ever since that day and the argument with my mother, our relations had soured. Two or three weeks later our door-bell rang, and Grandmother and Fereshteh came for a visit. Mother who was watering the garden was taken by surprise. She was still upset, but she couldn't and didn't dare to be disrespectful, especially towards Grandmother.

Father ran forwards and greeted them and invited them inside the house. But Grandmother said, 'No, it's better out here. It's almost pleasant sitting in the garden now.' Letting her chador fall on to her shoulders, she sat on the bench in the corner where Mother had spread a rug. Fereshteh entered the house and picked up Shadi and kissed her. The attention she paid to Shadi upset me very much. She spoke to Arash and didn't even notice me.

Miserable and upset I went up the stairs. I didn't feel like going to my room. The door at the top of the stairs leading to the terrace had been left open because the weather had suddenly turned warm. I slowly passed by the obstacles Mother had laid out to prevent Shadi from going up there. I went outside and reached the railing, lay on the ground so they wouldn't see me and looked at them from under the bars. Mother brought them juice, fruit and some plates. Then she gathered the glasses. Grandmother said, 'Come, sit down. Why do you keep moving around so much? We didn't mean to trouble you.'

My mother said something and went back inside.

Asi said, 'Look how dumb they are. She isn't going back and forth to serve them. She's just trying to avoid them.'

Mother returned and held the tea-tray in front of Grandmother, who took this opportunity to say, 'I heard you got upset because the kids teased one another and now you don't visit any more.'

Father said, 'No, Mother, that's not it at all. I'm just very busy and don't have much time to visit. Believe me, I hardly see my own children.'

'Why do you work so hard? If you were a bit thriftier and saved, you wouldn't need to work so hard. I'm worried about you.'

'It's not about being thrifty. Raising three kids costs money. And we lost Maryam's income when she stopped working after Shadi was born.'

'What women earn doesn't matter that much; it all gets spent on beauty salons, entertainment and nannies anyway. You two brothers shouldn't be cross with each other. If Hossein said anything, it was out of concern. He only said you should take the child to a doctor.'

Trying to keep her voice calm and respectful, my mother answered, 'We've taken Shahaab to the doctor many times and every time they've told us there's nothing wrong with him. Many children start speaking later for various reasons.'

'Is that right? Well, the doctor doesn't understand anything. Take him to see a better doctor. It's not possible for a normal child his age not to speak a word. Maybe if you deal with it sooner you'll be able to do something about it.'

'Don't worry yourself. There's nothing wrong with him. We'll take care of it ourselves.'

'Sweetheart, you have your head in the sand. Do you mean to say he isn't retarded in any way?'

'No. He's actually pretty clever.'

'Really! I don't know about you, but I've never seen such a thing in my life.'

'I've seen many children who started speaking late and had no problems.'

'Darling, the things you're saying show that you can't accept the truth. I've heard there are schools for retarded kids. Maybe if he goes to one sooner they'll be able to help him.'

My mother's voice grew harsh, 'He is not retarded!' She angrily picked up the tea-cups and went inside. I knew she'd gone to the kitchen to cry.

At that moment I felt a great hatred towards my grandmother that would stay with me for ever. I wanted to tear her head off. I looked around but there wasn't anything on the terrace.

Asi said, 'We have to deal with her.'

Grandmother said in an indignant tone, 'Did you see that? Did you see how your wife responds to our kindness? You're proud of your educated wife but who knows where she's from? Who has this kid taken after anyway? If you'd married your cousin at least we would have known her entire family. Your uncle would have helped you out and you wouldn't have to work like a dog now. But no, you had to fall in love! How could you fall in love with this darkie anyway? They put a spell on you. I knew it, but no one listened to me!'

'That's enough, Mother. Maryam wasn't being disrespectful. You won't find anyone more gracious than her.'

'Didn't you see how she answered back?'

'She didn't say anything. She just said we'd taken him to the doctor and there's nothing wrong with him.'

'No, she can't stand me. Fataneh invites me over seven days a week, but I don't dare come over here even once a month.'

Mother who had arrived with the tea-tray heard this remark, and on the verge of tears said, 'You don't like coming here your-self. You're always welcome here, but you prefer going to their house instead. After all, she's your niece and you have a lot to say to each other.' She ran back inside to keep from bursting into tears.

I looked around once more. Asi was angry and Babi was sad. I noticed a brick that was keeping the terrace door ajar. I quietly crawled backwards. I got up and hunched over, went and picked up the brick. It was heavy. I lifted it with both hands, placed it near the railing and lay back on the ground. I pushed the brick under the bars and slid it to the edge of the terrace. It wobbled a bit and I pressed down on it with my hand to keep it from falling.

Grandmother said, 'Tell me if I'm wrong, but if you'd married your cousin, you wouldn't be facing any of these problems now. You wouldn't be so detached from us, wouldn't have this sick child and wouldn't need to work so hard.'

'That's enough, Mother! I wouldn't work with my uncle in the bazaar in a hundred years. Can't you give up complaining after all this time?'

'I can't help it. It upsets me when I see you so miserable.'

'I'm not miserable, Mother! I am very happy with my life. Stop worrying about me.'

'Happy with a retarded child? Working as hard as you do?'

Asi said, 'Move the brick over her head. Now aim well!'

Babi exclaimed fearfully, 'How do people die?'

Asi said, 'Like in the movies. They get hurt then they fall asleep. At least she won't talk any more. Now you be quiet too. Don't be so afraid. It'll feel good to get even.'

I pushed the brick forwards a bit more.

Babi said, 'Don't do it!'

Asi said, 'Lift your hand.'

The brick was heavier now and my small hands couldn't hold on to it any longer. It slipped out of my grip. Babi shut his eyes out of fear. The brick spun in the air, moving towards Grandmother's black, white and henna-coloured head.

CHAPTER 4

Chaos broke out with the sound of the falling brick and my grandmother's screams. I ran like the wind and rushed down the stairs. As I was about to enter the bathroom I came face to face with my mother who was hurrying out of the kitchen. I couldn't stop. I ran into the bathroom, went on tiptoes, locked the door and leaned against it. I was gasping for breath and could hear my heart hammering. I waited for the voices outside to become clearer. Someone asked for water. Mother rushed into the kitchen and came right back. I could hear Father's footsteps behind her. She asked, 'What happened?'

'A huge brick came out of nowhere and hit her on the head!'

'Who could have done such a thing?'

'Maybe it was your crazy child again! I'll kill him this time. Hurry up and take her some water. Where's the rubbing alcohol?'

I was shaking behind the bathroom door. Babi said, 'We did a very bad thing. They'll kill us when they find out it was us. Arash's father will kill us.'

Asi was shaken up and whispered, 'We didn't do it. It fell by itself. Isn't that right, Shahaab? It slipped out of your hand and fell.'

I didn't know what to do. I was terrified. The sounds outside caught my attention again. Everyone was running around. I recognized Arash's and Shadi's footsteps. My parents returned to the kitchen. Father said, 'Add more sugar.'

'Thank God it isn't anything serious, just a few scratches on her face.'

'A few? Her entire face is badly scratched and she has a bruised shoulder! She's twisted up in agony.'

'Thank God it didn't hit her on the head, who knows what would have happened then.'

'If I find that kid I'll rip him apart.'

My heart was beating wildly and cold sweat was running down my back.

'What kid?'

'Stop acting stupid. You know it must have been your crazy son.'

'That's enough! Stop making things up. The child was right here with me. I took him to the bathroom. Oh, I totally forgot! He's been in there for ages now!'

I was shocked. I put my hand in front of my mouth to keep from screaming for joy.

Asi said, 'Mother is such a liar!'

Father replied impatiently, 'Stop lying. Who else could it have been?'

'How should I know? We don't even have any bricks in our house. You saw the pieces. It must have been a brick. Maybe it detached and fell from the edge of the terrace. The poor child's been in the bathroom all this time. You can't find anyone else to blame, can you?'

I heard Uncle Hossein's voice. Babi said, 'Where did he come from? He got here fast!'

Uncle Hossein hurried into the kitchen and said, 'Nasser, where are you? Do you have any painkillers? She's in a lot of pain.'

'Let's take her to the hospital. They'll give her something if necessary.'

'Did you figure out who it was? Did you find Shahaab?'

Mother snapped, 'What's it got to do with Shahaab?'

'It must have been him. No sane person would do such a thing.'

'Stop blaming the poor child. He was right here with me. He gets blamed for everything around here since he can't talk and defend himself!'

'How can a brick fall out of nowhere?'

'The bricks on the edge of the terrace are loose and every once in a while one of them falls. Or maybe someone threw it from a neighbour's house, or from the street.'

I laughed uncontrollably. My heart calmed down and I could breathe again. I still had someone on my side!

Babi said, 'Mother is such a clever liar. I love her.'

Fereshteh yelled, 'Hurry up! She's in a lot of pain. We should take her to the hospital.'

'Hand me that sugar water. Let's go.'

They all rushed back to the garden screaming like a flock of birds.

The voices quietened down once Father's car had left. I took a deep breath but my legs didn't have the strength to support me any more. I slid on to the floor still leaning against the door. I said to my friends, 'It's nice to have a lying Mother. That's why I love her so much.'

The house was completely silent. Suddenly I was gripped with my usual fear. What if they had all gone and left me behind? The fear of being alone scared me even more than the fear of being told off and smacked. I was always anticipating the day when they would leave me behind and go away. I took a breath when I saw the door handle turning. Thank God I wasn't alone!

Mother said in a quiet voice, 'Open the door. They're gone.' She sounded so tired. After all the excitement I was very tired too. I wasn't afraid of Mother or her punishment. I unlocked the door with difficulty. She was sitting by the door, very pale, and burst into tears as soon as she saw me. I wasn't sure if I should feel sorrier for myself or for her. She took my hand and pulled me towards her. I stood in front of her and looked down. She said in a sad voice, 'Why did you do such a thing? She could have died if it had hit her on the head, and they would have taken you to prison. They would have locked you up in a small room all by yourself. You should know that what you did was very dangerous. Why don't you understand?'

I loved her so much. I hugged her and began to cry. I wished I could tell her that if anyone ever said anything bad about her, I would do that dangerous thing again. I wished I could tell her I loved her, that I was so happy to have a lying mother just like her.

CHAPTER 5

Everyone in my family is clever except for me. Arash is a lot older than I am. Mother says he'd just started school when I was born. He's a good boy and the family's source of pride. He's looked the same since he was a baby. He isn't tall, but he's thin, with white skin, dark hair and dark eyes. If he had a moustache he would look just like his father. Just like him, he is serious, buttoned up and self-centred. He always looks a bit sad. He didn't want anything to do with me even when we were younger. He was always busy reading or writing. His father looked at him with admiration. Instead, he always looked at me with a scowl on his face. He couldn't help it. It saddened him to look at me.

Shadi is my sister. She's more than a couple of years younger, but she's been babbling ever since I can remember. It's as if she knew how to talk since birth, exactly my opposite! She would open her mouth and say what she wanted to say. It really pissed me off. She wasn't afraid, her voice never shook and she wasn't embarrassed either. My mother cooed whenever she talked. She would call her 'the joy of my life'.* Shadi was the joy of her life, just as I was the sorrow of her life. She always said, 'My sorrow over him will be the end of me.' It feels terrible to know you're

* *Shadi* means 'joy' in Farsi.

24

causing your family sadness. Sometimes I wanted to rip Shadi's head off. But she always screamed before I could reach her and Mother would arrive breathlessly. I, however, could never complain no matter how much she pestered me.

The only good thing about Shadi's birth was that Mother stopped going to work for a few years and Akram stopped coming to our house. Before Shadi was born, they would all get ready in the morning and leave me crying with Akram. They pretended they would be back very soon, but they didn't realize how slowly time passed for me back then. Every day I would think that they had gone and left me with Akram for good. My heart would be filled with anxiety until they got back in the evening.

Mother liked Akram. She said she was a good woman. Maybe she was. She helped Mother, swept the house all the time and washed me several times a day. The unfortunate woman had a cleaning fetish, though, and it was more unfortunate for me because I had to shine like a brand-new doll. She didn't know anything about playing; I was either supposed to eat, sleep, or sit in my cot with its high rail. If I got a single spot on my clothes she would pull at her cheeks and say, 'Oh my God!', and look at me and the spot as if I were a most disgusting thing. It scared me.

She was always singing sad songs. Sometimes when she was in a good mood she would talk to me, but in a language that only she understood. She would use different names for the things I was just beginning to learn and this confused me. She would speak the same way with the neighbour while hanging clothes on the balcony. Sometimes she would bring her daughter with her and on those days their language was the only thing spoken in the house. They would stop as soon as my mother arrived. Words would suddenly change and I didn't understand why something that was called *sou** all day would suddenly be called 'water'.

All this changed with Shadi's arrival. Mother stopped going to work. Even though she spent most of her time with Shadi and would do homework with Arash once he got back from school,

---

* *Sou* is Turkish for 'water'.

I still liked that she was around. I stopped crying every day. It was enough to know she was there, and that I could look at her whenever I wanted to. I can still see her beautiful young face, her olive skin and large hazel eyes, the thick dark hair she often tied back, and her white teeth and pleasant smile that I loved more than anything else in the world.

The most important person in our house was Arash's father. He would leave the house noisily in the mornings and I would try to stay asleep until he left. It would be dark by the time he came back. He probably worked several jobs, and always seemed tired. His black moustache looked droopier in the evenings. He would sleep in front of the TV until supper time. Then he would eat in silence, grab his newspaper, and say goodnight. He would slowly go up the stairs to their bedroom, which used to be across from Shadi's and mine (it has now moved downstairs). He always complained that he couldn't sleep.

Mother would start talking as soon as Arash's father came home. 'What's up? How was your day?' But he would respond in a serious tone, 'Nothing, same as always, work, work, work.'

'What's wrong? Aren't you feeling well?'

'Stop questioning me. I'm just tired.'

I could feel that this upset her but she wouldn't say anything. I don't know if it was pride or shyness that made her stop asking.

Arash was the only one allowed to disturb his father's peace and quiet. He would ask him questions about his homework. The more difficult the questions, the happier his father was. Then he would look at Mother with pride and say, 'See how clever my son is?' Sometimes he would look at me and say, 'Remember how many songs Arash could sing when he was this age?'

I knew what he meant. He was pointing out my stupidity and humiliating Mother. They talked about the issue of my speech all the time, and sometimes tried to force me to speak. All this attention scared me even more. I would feel sick and my heart would start to race. I wanted to run away and hide in a dark room. I would go and hunch over in a corner, but everyone kept talking in my head. Babi would be sad that he wasn't as smart as Arash and not loved by Father.

Asi would angrily say, 'The hell with him. I want to beat them all up. What good is he anyway? He can get lost as far as I'm concerned. I don't love any of them.'

Babi would say, 'But I love Mother.'

Asi hated Arash's father more and more each day. And my tongue grew heavier and heavier as I understood the extent of my dumbness and knew I would never be able to speak.

Asi and Babi were the only ones who understood me and loved me the way I was. Their presence was a godsend. I wasn't sure if they were a boy or a girl, but it didn't make a difference, they were exactly as they should be. I could talk and play with them for hours.

CHAPTER 6

One month had passed since the attempt on Grandmother's life, but she still winced in pain, especially whenever she saw my parents. She would say, 'I can't move my hands. I've become a cripple.'

Asi didn't believe a word she said. He would whisper meanly, 'She's lying. I saw her washing for prayer using both hands.'

I had mixed feelings about what I'd done. Despite the immense fear I felt afterwards, and the consequences, I didn't really regret it. Like an honest judge who believes he's given the right verdict, my conscience felt clear. I was sure that Father somehow knew the truth, and I was sort of happy about this, but nonetheless, I tried to hide from him for a few days.

Grandmother moved to Uncle Hossein's house for a while, and my mother and Fataneh divided the responsibility of caring for her between them. Inevitably the relations between the two families resumed. Fataneh kept asking Mother, 'Maryam, did you finally figure out where the brick came from?'

My mother would confidently reply, 'Someone must have thrown it from the street. We don't have any bricks in our house.'

I lived in peace and calm in those days. The revenge I'd taken had calmed me for a while. Mother had lied on my behalf and I tried to be a good boy and stay close to her as she'd asked. But

Khosrow was bent on finding me by myself and every time he passed by he would say, 'How are you doing, dummy?' I really wanted to attack him, but I held back. I just spat on him a few times, and each time he ran to his mother screaming, 'See what the psycho did!'

Fataneh, shaking her head, would shoot a meaningful glance at my mother, and Mother would say, 'Khosrow it's your own fault for annoying him. You must have done something to him and since he can't talk, this is how he defends himself.'

Fataneh would get irate and say to Khosrow, 'Just stay away from him so they stop blaming you.'

One day Fataneh and Mother decided to give Grandmother a bath. The women went into the bathroom and Mother said to me, 'Sit here till I get back. Don't go anywhere!'

I sat behind the bathroom door. Shadi was talking in Fereshteh's room. Fereshteh laughed with joy. My heart felt squeezed.

Babi said, 'Shadi's taken Fereshteh away from us with all her babbling. She doesn't love us any more and hasn't hugged us in a long time. She doesn't like us going into her room either and only takes Shadi there.'

I was bored and felt sorry for myself.

Asi said, 'How long are they going to take with this bath?'

I realized Khosrow was calling me from upstairs, 'Shahaab, come up here, I want to show you something.'

I knew he had a trick up his sleeve, but I was curious. I slowly went up the stairs. Their house was identical to ours. All the houses on this street were built in the same style, with the living room, dining room and an extra room on the lower level, and two bedrooms and a terrace upstairs. Khosrow's room was messy as always, with paper and card strewn all around, and a large pot of glue on his desk. It looked like he was trying to make a kite. I entered the room cautiously.

Khosrow shut the door behind me and said, 'Sit on the bed.' Then he pulled open his desk drawer and took out a cigarette and matches. It was like he was showing off a treasure. He

29

boasted, 'Do you know what this is? It's a cigarette. It's so good. I'm going to be a smoker when I grow up. I even know how to smoke now. Just watch.' He struck a match. I stared at its bluish-yellow flame. He placed the cigarette between his lips and lit it. A white smoke filled the room and the space started to smell like my uncle. Then the smoke went out of the open window. Khosrow closed his eyes and said, 'It's amazing. Here, you try.' I turned my head around and pushed Khosrow away. 'Scaredy-cat! No one will find out. Just take a puff. Don't worry, if it was bad I wouldn't do it myself.'

I looked at the rising smoke, amazed by this magical feat. Khosrow carefully placed the cigarette between my lips and said, 'Pretend you're drinking from a straw and suck hard.' I sucked on the cigarette with all my might. Smoke filled my entire being. I could feel my brain getting hot, and felt the thick, stinking smoke all through my body. I started to cough and couldn't breathe. I began to go blue and my eyes felt like they were about to pop out of my head. My guts were coming out of me. I threw up and fainted on the floor.

Khosrow screamed, '*Get lost, you filthy leech! Look what you did to my room!*' And he ran down the stairs. I came to at last and followed him shakily.

Mother rushed out of the bathroom terrified and wet with sweat. Fataneh peered out too, and Khosrow said with disgust, 'The idiot threw up in my room. All my things are ruined.'

Fataneh pursed her lips with loathing and said, 'You know this kid isn't normal and can't control himself. Why did you take him to your room?'

Mother said, 'He never throws up for no reason. He must be ill.' She walked towards where I was standing by the stairs, limp and pale. She felt my forehead and asked, 'Why did you get sick, sweetheart?' She liked to talk to me in front of other people as if I could answer her.

Fataneh brought Grandmother out of the bathroom and helped her sit down. Her clothes were wet and wrinkled like my mother's.

Asi said, 'The brick didn't hit her on the legs. So why is she limping like that? She's nasty!'

Fataneh went to the kitchen and came back with a broom, some rags and a pail of water. Her lips were still pressed together in disgust. Mother said, 'Give those to me. I'll clean it up.' Fataneh handed them over as if she was waiting for these words.

I held on to Mother's skirt and went upstairs with her. I couldn't stand the rebuking glances of my grandmother and the others for one more second. She shut the door and started cleaning the rug. She was frowning, and looked sad and tired.

Babi said, 'See how we made her cry again.'

I wanted to rip off Khosrow's head. I looked around and noticed the pot of glue on his desk. There was a brush inside it. I took it and brushed it over the entire surface of the desk and everything on it. Mother was so sad and busy working that she didn't notice me. She looked up once and I stood in front of the glue pot, scared. Without paying any attention she just said, 'Why are you standing there? Go and sit down.' She lowered her head again. I picked up the pot and hid it behind me, and stepping backwards went and sat on the bed. I lifted the covers and poured glue all over the bed. Then I took the clothes that were strewn over the bed and shoved them under the covers. Mother was done cleaning and said, 'Come on, let's go. We're done for today.' I innocently took the edge of her skirt and went down the stairs.

We went home early that day. Mother went to take a shower and I ran to my room. I shut the door on Shadi who was following me. I joined hands with Asi and Babi and we circled the room until we grew dizzy. It felt great.

The next day Fataneh told Mother about the glue, the dirty bed and all the clothes they had had to throw away. Mother simply asked, 'Why did Khosrow put the glue pot in his bed?'

Everyone was apparently waiting for this question and they all began talking at once, but Fataneh's voice could be heard over everyone else's, 'That's just it. He says he didn't do it. We need to find out who was in Khosrow's room that day.'

Mother was incensed, 'What do you mean? I went in his room to clean up. Do you mean to say I—?'

'No, not you, but maybe the children were there with you and did it without you noticing.'

'You mean Shahaab? Impossible. I was watching him the entire time. I didn't leave him alone for even a moment. It wasn't him. I am sure of it.'

She turned and looked at me and her gaze began to waver with doubt. She shook her head as if to send away the bad thought that had crept into her head.

CHAPTER 7

In those days I couldn't understand Shahaab at all. My quiet son had suddenly transformed into a complicated, unpredictable boy who did strange things.

I wondered whether I should punish him, or if he was really retarded, and if we had failed in his upbringing. I had sacrificed my whole life for my family. I worked day and night in that house just like a maid. So what was he missing? Why weren't Arash and Shadi the same way? Arash was a good student, polite, always top of his year. He had never caused more trouble than was usual for any child. And Shadi was as sweet as honey, smart and talkative. Thank goodness for her, otherwise I would have gone mad from my monotonous life and my sadness over Shahaab.

I couldn't stand Nasser any more. Sometimes I thought he couldn't stand us either. I would try to remember the feelings that had led to our marriage, the time filled with stupid dreams, when we thought we could conquer the world just by having a Bachelor's degree in chemistry. The days when the stress of an exam would mix with the anxiety of being in love; when I would leave my digs in the mornings not sure which was causing the butterflies in my stomach. Where had those feelings gone? Those days seemed so far away. I would search the depths of my heart, like looking for an old piece of clothing in an abandoned cupboard. I would eventually find it with surprise, but it was hardly recognizable any more, faded and covered in dust. I didn't even want to touch it again. Is this all I expected from life? Me, Ahmad Ali Khan's one and only daughter, with all my airs? The one who wanted to prove she was no less than any boy? I, who hated my mother's life because I witnessed her serving her husband and five rowdy sons all day long? I had studied more than my brothers, and worked harder than anyone else at the office, trying to gain everyone's approval. When had I become an ordinary housewife? This wasn't the life I had planned for myself. Why did I lose all my dreams and hopes? For whom? Did this faded love deserve such sacrifice? Sometimes I felt miles away from Nasser. He didn't notice me any longer and was always tired or sad. As Shahaab's problems grew worse it felt like our relationship became cooler, as if I were responsible for his lack of speech.

CHAPTER 8

I had learned how to take revenge on those who called me dumb or stupid. It would calm me down, and then I could play with Asi and Babi again. The three of us would run around the room and laugh. They punished me but it didn't matter. Ever since Arash's father had given me a hiding and locked me in my room for an entire day and night for shredding his suits with a pair of scissors, I had stopped being scared of anything. It couldn't get any worse than that.

I wanted to be able to swear. All the other kids did it, and I wanted to repeat those magical words too! Back then I didn't understand why I wanted to swear so badly, but I felt it was a great way for getting even. You didn't need to be powerful or big and strong to use bad language, you just needed to know how to speak, to open your mouth and say something to make the other person mad. Words could be powerful. If you used the right word at the right time you could make people fume with anger without having to break or destroy anything. It was as if those words had been invented for small, weak people like myself.

I could recognize swear words. I would carefully listen to them and memorize them. Sometimes I knew what they meant, like *pedar-sag** for instance. Once when Arash's father was cross with

---

* *Pedar-sag* literally means: 'Your father is a dog.'

him he told Mother, 'Tell that *pedar-sag* that I've had it with his rotten behaviour.'

The fact that he was mad at Arash was strange in itself, but his use of a swear word was even odder.

We went to our room. Asi said, 'Arash's father swore!'

Babi said, 'Yes, he said his father is a dog!'

I said, 'That means he's a dog himself!'

We laughed our heads off that day. We circled the room singing '*pedar-sag, pedar-sag . . .*'

But there were some words I didn't understand at all, and I couldn't figure out why people got cross when they heard them. One day one of the kids told Khosrow, 'Your mother is brown.'* They got into a fight and beat each other up.

I tried to figure out what this meant and why it was a bad thing for someone's mother to be brown.

Babi said, 'Brown is a colour. Maybe his mother always wears brown.'

Asi said, 'So what? What's wrong with that? A lot of women wear brown.'

'Maybe he hates that colour.'

I said, 'I hate it too. I want Mother to wear pink all the time, but I wouldn't get this angry if she wore something brown.'

We were confused for a while. Then Asi said, 'Maybe he means coffee.'

Sometimes Fataneh would come to our house to gossip about Grandmother and my uncle. Mother would make coffee and they would drink it all, never giving us any. She said it wasn't good for kids. Then they would look at their empty cups and talk rubbish. One time Fataneh told Mother, 'In either two weeks or two months from now, something will make you very happy.'

Mother got very excited, 'Are you sure? Maybe Shahaab will start speaking!'

* In Farsi the word for brown (which is the same word as coffee) sounds similar to the word for 'whore'.

36

I don't know why everything always ended up being about my speech. Fataneh pursed her lips and said, 'I don't think so. It seems to be about finances. You'll probably come into some money.' Mother looked sad again.

Asi said, 'Coffee is a bad thing. They look at their cups and talk rubbish. Mothers shouldn't drink coffee. Why doesn't Arash's father ever have any? Or uncle? This is a bad thing that mothers do and that's why they never let us have any.'

Babi said, 'We should do something so Mother stops drinking coffee.'

A few days later we were playing in my room when we smelled coffee. We peeked from the stairs and saw Fataneh and Mother sitting in the hall, drinking coffee. Right then Khosrow walked in. My heart clenched. Asi said, 'What's he going to do if he sees them drinking coffee?'

I ran down the stairs and reached the table. Like a determined grown-up scolding a smaller child I threw everything off the table. The cups broke and some coffee spilled on Fataneh. She screamed and said, 'What's wrong with you?'

Mother just looked at me in confusion and then said angrily, 'What's got into you? Why did you do this? Are you mad?'

Fataneh smirked, 'Is he mad? Of course he is! No normal kid would do such a thing.'

I looked at Khosrow waiting for him to reprimand them, but he was holding his belly and laughing hard. He finally said, 'I keep telling you he's mad and you keep denying it!'

I was very confused. Why wasn't he upset? Didn't he beat up that other kid over his mother drinking coffee?

Mother smacked the back of my head, yanked my ear, dragged me upstairs and locked me in my room. She said I wasn't allowed to come out until night-time. I was so confused I didn't even get cross. I wanted to be alone anyway.

After everyone left Asi said, 'So there was nothing wrong with coffee.'

Babi said, 'Then why is it a swear word?'

I said, 'Who knows.'

Asi said, 'I got it! Whatever you call someone's mother is a bad thing. Coffee isn't bad, but if you say, "Your mother is coffee", then it's bad.'

'So if we say, "Your mother is tea", is that bad too?'

'It must be very bad because tea can't be anyone's mother!'

'That's funny. Grown-ups are idiots! They make up such silly things.' The three of us laughed and laughed.

Asi used everything in the room to make a rude word and we found that even funnier. 'Your mother's a chair, your mother's a desk . . .'

Babi said, 'No, it has to be something you can eat or drink. Your mother's fried rice. Your mother's a stew.'

We found it so amusing we didn't notice Mother coming into the room. She looked at me with concern, 'What's wrong? Why are you laughing like that? Have you gone insane?'

I could see Fataneh's head behind her. I tried to keep from finding it funny. I put my hand in front of my mouth and kept quiet. But Asi wickedly whispered in my ear, 'Your mother's an eggplant.' I couldn't help it and burst out laughing.

Mother looked very worried. 'Stop laughing like that – you're scaring me. Fataneh what's happening? I shouldn't have hit him so hard. I shouldn't have locked him up. It's probably affected him.'

Mother kept watching me all day and I had to be careful not to laugh in front of her.

Asi said, 'These grown-ups are really stupid. Why is she afraid of a laughing child?'

That night when Arash's dad came home, Mother told him the whole story. She told him what I'd done, and that I'd been scolded and locked up afterwards, and how instead of crying and being sad, I'd laughed. Arash's dad shook his head and said, 'We have to find a specialist. It's becoming more and more serious every day. This is a bad sign.'

Mother became tearful and said, 'Really? Do you think he has a psychological problem?'

'Could it be anything else?'

'Maybe something made him happy. I wish he could tell us what goes through his head.'

Babi said, 'She's so stupid. If we could talk we would just ask what a "brown mother" means and wouldn't break the dishes over nothing.'

I finally gave up, and decided not to look for a meaning for swear words. After all, I was dumb and couldn't understand these things. Furthermore, I didn't really need to know what such words meant, I just had to know whether they meant something very rude. And I could figure this out from the level of anger they caused. For instance, a few weeks later when Mother and I were at the butcher's, someone was angrily describing something to Mr Sadegh. The man said, 'If I could only catch that pimp!' I recognized this had to be a swear word. I looked at Mother, who blushed and wanted to leave the shop.

Mr Sadegh said, 'Watch your mouth, there's a lady present,' and apologized to Mother. I realized that this was indeed a very rude word. I repeated it in my head all the way back home; so much power for such a small word! It sounded nice too. It felt small and round, and jumped out of your mouth like a marble.

Babi said, 'What does it mean?'

'It doesn't mean anything. It's just very bad, kind of like the "brown mother" thing. Women shouldn't hear it. Didn't you know? Swear words that are about animals aren't that bad, but the ones that don't mean anything are very, very bad. If you say any of these words all of the women will run out of the room and the men will get so angry they'll start fighting.'

That day Asi, Babi and I circled the room for hours and repeated this word that sounded like a bright pink and blue marble.

CHAPTER 9

A miracle occurred that summer which took the insane amount of attention off me. My Aunt Shahin was getting married and her hurried wedding plans became the focus. Everyone was happy and kept talking about the marriage. Mother, Fataneh, Grandmother and Aunt Shahin would sit for hours discussing the wedding dress, the rehearsal supper and all sorts of other things. Fataneh was a good seamstress and Mother knew how to apply sequins. The two of them worked on the wedding dress and the room where they worked was filled with white satin and lace; soft delicate fabrics that Fataneh's and Mother's magic fingers turned into amazing dresses I'd only seen in cartoons and picture books. I loved the pristine whiteness and beauty of these fabrics, and I burned with envy when I realized they had made a small wedding dress for Shadi too.

Babi said, 'Good for her. Everyone likes her because she can talk, but no one likes us.'

We went to my uncle's house every day to work on the dress. It was two days before the wedding and I didn't feel too well. Mother said, 'He's caught a cold.' She placed her cool hand against my forehead. 'He has a fever, I can't leave him alone. He needs to rest.'

Father, irritable as always, replied, 'Today of all days! It's the henna ceremony and they need you over there! My mother said the dress wasn't ready either. She's worried it won't be finished in just two days. If you don't go over today they'll give you a hard time for the rest of your life.'

'I know. I'll go. I just wish Arash would stay at home today so I could leave Shahaab and let him rest.'

'That's impossible! Arash can't miss school for him. He's not your child's nanny. You said Fereshteh would take care of Shadi, so she won't be a problem. Take him with you and let him sleep in a corner somewhere.'

He always called me 'him', as if I didn't have a name. I hated it when he talked this way.

Mother laid me down on a sofa in the hall, set busily to work and forgot all about me. The hours dragged by slowly. I was bored. I sat in front of the TV for a while, fell asleep, woke up and it was finally time for lunch. After lunch they all gathered in the kitchen to wash the dishes. I wanted to stay next to Mother but she sent me out of the kitchen and said, 'Go on, get out of the way, love. Go and lie down, and I'll be right there.'

I felt tired. I knew she would go back to the room where they were making the dress. I opened the door. The dress was laid out on the floor. I sat down next to it and took hold of a corner of it. I pressed my face against the material. It felt soft and cool, just like my velvet blanket at home. The skirt of the dress was so big that my entire body fitted over it. I sat in the centre of the skirt and wrapped the rest of the fabric around my legs. A pleasant coolness spread over my body. My feverish eyes grew heavy. I lay my head down in the folds of the dress and fell into a deep sleep.

I woke up in terror to Aunt Shahin's screams. All the women were standing over me, looking at me with hateful, angry eyes. I began to shiver. Any one of them might strangle me at that moment. After a few seconds their cold, bitter gaze turned to Mother, who was standing by the door. I could feel her shaking too.

Grandmother said in her harsh voice, 'See what he's done! The entire dress is stained and wrinkled. Look at his footprints!'

41

My aunt began to cry.

Fataneh said, 'I knew he would do something like this.'

Mother just looked on in confusion. Her face had turned pale. She stepped forwards, picked up the dress and examined it. 'I'll repair it myself. It'll be as good as new. I promise.'

'There's no need! I'm worried you'll make it worse. We'll fix it ourselves.'

'You don't have time. Didn't you want to go to the hairdresser? And you have a lot of guests tonight. I'll take it home, finish it and return it as good as new. Don't worry. I'll remove the stains with some foam and I'll iron it. Don't distress yourselves.'

Shadi was having a nap in Fereshteh's room, so Mother and I went back home, carrying the dress in a large plastic bag. She washed the dress in silence and let it dry. I hated that dress, Aunt Shahin and her wedding.

Asi said, 'Why are they so stupid? Why don't they realize we didn't want to ruin the dress, we just fell asleep on it?'

Mother hung the dress from the door. She sat down in front of it and finished the sequins. She looked upset. The phone rang. She got up to answer it and I could hear her voice saying, 'Don't worry, it looks fine. There is no sign of the stains. Please don't say anything. He didn't do it on purpose, believe me. He is ill and was sleepy. He just wanted to rest on it.'

The voices at the other end led to my mother's soundless weeping. I felt a great hatred inside me. Why did they keep making her cry? She seemed to be getting more and more helpless every day, which made me even angrier. I looked around. I saw a pair of scissors on the floor. I picked them up. They were heavy and big for my small hands. I opened them with difficulty, placed the fabric of the dress between the blades, and pressed them together. After a few snips a large hole appeared in the dress.

Asi said, 'Now, that'll show them!'

Babi was worried and said, 'What will Aunt Shahin wear now?'

Asi said, 'They deserve it for making Mother cry.'

CHAPTER 10

I screamed uncontrollably when I saw the hole in the dress. Hearing me, Shahaab dropped the scissors. I was quivering all over as though I were connected to a live wire. I put my hands over my mouth to stop screaming, while my eyes were popping out of my skull. I said, 'Oh my God! What have you done!' and charged towards him. He ran for the stairs as fast as his little legs could carry him. He rushed upstairs, shut the door and tried to lock it, but I knew he couldn't do it. I ran after him with shaking legs. I only made it halfway up the stairs and had to hang on to the banister to regain my balance. I yelled, 'Come down here, you rascal! What am I going to do with you? You'll be the death of me.' After a bit of yelling and screaming all my anger was drained and I was on the verge of tears. I sat on the stairs, put my head in my hands and began to cry. I don't know how long I had been weeping when I felt Shahaab's small, light hand on my hair. I knew that he couldn't bear to see me cry, but I didn't realize he was even willing to be punished and smacked to stop me from crying.

What was I supposed to do with him? I looked at him. His large hazel eyes were filled with tears, and the sadness on his face made my stomach clench. He was in pain too and I could feel it. I hugged him and said, 'Why? Why do you cause so much

trouble? You used to be such a good boy. What happened to you?'
He hung his head. 'I know you do all these things out of spite,
but this will only make things worse. Do you realize what you
just did to me? Do you think you only hurt Aunt Shahin? With
every bad thing you do, you hurt me more than anyone else.
Don't you love me? Don't you?'

He burst out crying and tears streamed down his face. He hid
himself in my arms. 'If you love me, just stop doing these things.
Tell me if anyone bothers you and I'll deal with them myself.
You don't need to do anything.' He looked at me quizzically and
I realized my mistake. 'No, you don't need to say anything. I'll
find out if anyone bothers you, and more importantly, God will
see and hear everything too, and will teach them a lesson better
than you can. He will take care of you. Just control yourself, and
let God and me handle everything, okay? Will you promise? If
you only love me a little bit you'll stop doing these things. Otherwise I'll die from sadness. I almost died when I saw the dress just
now. Do you want me to die? Then you won't have a mother any
more.'

He pressed his head against my shoulder. I gently unwrapped
his hands from around my neck, looked into his eyes and said,
'Then you promise? Right?' He nodded his head. 'You promise
that if anyone hurts you, you'll come straight to me?' He nodded
again. We both felt calmer.

I got up and went back to the dress. I looked at the hole in
fear. The only option was to separate the skirt from the top and
replace the damaged piece. I went to the kitchen and poured
myself some tea to regain some of my lost energy. After a few
minutes I suddenly jumped up. Where was Shahaab? What if
he was causing more trouble? I ran back to the room and saw
him trying to tape back the cut-out piece with his small hands.
My eyes filled with tears and I said, 'It won't work this way,
darling. Don't worry about it. I know what to do so no one will
find out.'

I took the hanger off the door, grabbed the dress and began
unstitching the skirt. He sat next to me and watched me with

curiosity and worry. I spread out the skirt on the floor. Its many folds opened up and I saw that the damaged piece was next to a seam. I cut out a long strip of the fabric and gave it to Shahaab. 'Here you are, but make sure no one sees it.' But he scrunched up the fabric in disgust and threw it in the bin. I brought the sewing machine and started to fold the skirt and sew the seam.

At the sound of the garage door opening Shahaab ran to the window. I whispered, 'Go to your room and lie down.' He ran up the stairs. Nasser and Arash walked in. I tried to act naturally and said, 'You're home early today!'

'You asked me to pick Arash up and come home early so we would get to the henna ceremony.'

'I know, but I thought you'd forget.'

'What are you doing? Isn't the dress done yet?'

'It is, but it got stained a bit. I brought it over to clean, but it got worse. I had to replace a piece. The dress has so many folds that no one will notice. Just be careful you don't blurt anything out.'

'You're so careless! You're as bad as your child.'

'What do you mean, careless? Accidents happen. I was worried about Shahaab.'

'Why? Did anything happen again?'

'No, it's just that he's ill. I'm worried about him. He's been sleeping all day.'

'That's a relief. At least he didn't cause more trouble. You should start getting ready if you want to get to the ceremony on time.'

'No, you go ahead. I have to finish the dress before anyone finds out.'

'What? What am I going to tell them? They need your help there.'

'They don't need my help. The best thing I can do for them is to finish this dress. We got everything done this morning. Akram and her daughter are coming to help too. Shadi stayed with Fereshteh. Go and pick her up, and tell them Shahaab's sick

45

and I have to stay with him. They'll be pleased if the kids aren't around anyway. If they need help serving supper, give me a call and we'll come over.'

Arash went and picked Shadi up, but he said that Fereshteh had begged him to take her back this evening because they had rehearsed a dance for the guests. I bathed her, dressed her and tied a pink ribbon around her beautiful hair. I put her in Nasser's arms and walked them to the door. When I turned around I saw Shahaab looking after them enviously.

It was dark when I finished repairing the dress, but I still had a lot more to do. I had to finish the sequins. I was tired and my eyes were weary. I was so deep in thought that I'd forgotten all about Shahaab, but he showed up carrying a bottle of water and two sweets. He ran back into the kitchen and brought a glass too. I realized that he somehow wanted to do something for me. I felt sorry for him. 'Do you want to help?' He nodded. I drank the water and with all my feelings of sadness and weariness I said, 'Your biggest help would be to talk to me. Just say one word. Say "Mum" . . . ' I wiped the tears from my cheeks and started work-ing on the dress again.

After a few moments I heard a soft voice filled with emotion, 'Mum!'

My heart started to beat fast and I looked at him in disbelief. 'What did you say? Was that you?' I placed my hands on his shoulders. Tears began to flow down my face again and I begged, 'Say it again, just one more time!' The phone rang and made me jump. I was still laughing and crying when I picked it up. 'Nasser, do you know what just happened? Shahaab just called me "Mum"! I swear it's the truth. He has such a beautiful voice. He just said "Mum" out of the blue . . . Yes, I'll be right over. Tell them not to serve supper till I get there to help. Yes, the dress is almost done. I'll bring it over tomorrow. We'll get dressed right away and come over.'

I took a quick shower and got dressed. I tied my wet hair in a knot and put on some light red lipstick. Shahaab looked at me with a sweet smile on his lips. My happiness always seemed to make him happy too, as if our souls were somehow tied together. I was so happy, I kept talking in a rush. 'Thank God! I knew it. I knew there was nothing wrong with you. Now I'll be redeemed in front of all of them, and they can stop their vicious gossip and innuendo.'

I grabbed his hand and proudly headed to Hossein's house.

CHAPTER 11

My mother's tired, stressed face had affected me so much I was willing to do anything to relieve her pain. This made me forget my fear of speaking; I opened my mouth and said easily, 'Mum'. The unfamiliar voice sounded strange to my ears. Was this really my voice? Her happiness pleased me. She looked so beautiful when she was happy. But bit by bit I began to fear her excitement and her unusual response. On the way over to Uncle's house, Asi said, 'Why did she tell Arash's father that we spoke? What if she tells the others too?'

I got scared and pulled my hand out of hers. I wanted to go back home. Mother looked at me with happiness. She took my hand again and said, 'Let's go, darling. Let's go, my sweet boy.'

They all turned quiet as soon as we walked in. These were people who usually didn't notice me but now they couldn't take their curious eyes off me. My heart began to pound. Even Mother was a bit surprised. Fataneh ran forwards maliciously. She knelt in front of me and said with a smile, 'Oh my God! Shahaab! I heard you could talk. Be a good boy and say "Fataneh", let me hear your voice.' Up close her face looked scary covered in make-up. I hid behind Mother. 'Go on, say something.'

I grew hot. Mother pulled my hand and said, 'Leave him alone. You're upsetting him.'

'Didn't you say he could talk? Well, I want to hear him say my name.'

'You're scaring him.'

'I'm not doing anything!'

Khosrow looked at me mockingly. Father stepped forwards. He brought his face closer to mine.

'Now that you've said "Mum", make me happy and say "Dad".'

Everyone was waiting. I felt like I couldn't breathe and my heart was beating faster. Mother, my only source of hope and protection, had betrayed me. She had told everyone something that was supposed to be our secret. I pulled my hand out of hers and ran towards our house, promising myself that I wouldn't make this mistake ever again, that I would never feel sorry for her.

The days passed by with everyone talking about me, and then, suddenly, it all came to an end. After a while everyone including Mother came to believe that she'd probably imagined it all out of her great desire to hear me speak. They left me alone, and once again I fell back into the safe world of my wordlessness.

CHAPTER 12

The first month of summer was all about the wedding and the parties that followed. Because of his multiple classes Arash had no time for these events and it seemed he didn't want to go anyway. He preferred to stay at home, read, watch TV, draw or do art projects. It seemed to me that he too was reluctant to communicate and talk to other people. His friend Saman, who was just like him and wore large glasses over his beady eyes, would often come over. They constantly talked about serious things, and to prove their theories they would dismantle radios and vacuum cleaners and other appliances, and of course no one considered this mischief! Father said, 'My son is experimenting. He's so smart – some day he'll invent something.'

Mother took advantage of Arash's presence at home and left me with him while she attended all the parties, taking Shadi with her. Arash usually left me to myself. Like Father, he didn't consider me worthy of his attention. They all ignored me in a way, which made me feel unwanted. As they got ready to go out a sense of excitement would take over the house and I would follow them from one room to the next. Mother would try on a few dresses, finally choosing one to wear. I wished she would do this all day long so I would never have to deal with the heavy silence that took over the house once they had left.

She would kiss me and say, 'That was delicious.' A delicious supper is what they bribed us with on the nights they went out. 'Sit down and draw something pretty when we leave, and then go to bed.'

But I didn't feel like doing anything in that silent house. I would just draw a few meaningless, nervous lines. Day by day I became more attached to my imaginary friends.

Asi said, 'Let them all go to hell.' But Babi was very sad.

CHAPTER 13

A strange thing happened towards evening one warm summer day. Fereshteh came over to our house. She had a pretty scarf on. Asi said, 'What has she done? She looks prettier.' Unlike her usual routine she didn't run to Shadi as soon as she walked in. Instead, she looked for me and called my name, like she used to do a long time ago. I stepped out from behind the door. She embraced me. I loved it when she hugged me. I took a deep breath of her perfume and listened in awe to what she said. She addressed me first, and then looked at Mother, 'Will you come to the park with me? Maryam, I want to take Shahaab out. Is that okay?'

Mother looked at her suspiciously, 'Shahaab! Why him?'

'What's wrong with that? I like him. Don't you remember how much I used to play with him? We'll just go for a stroll in the park and come right back.'

'No. I'm afraid something might happen and I'm really not in the mood for trouble. It's okay if you want to take Shadi with you, but not Shahaab. I'll be more comfortable if he stays here with me.'

'I swear I'll take care of him. Nothing's going to happen. I've been thinking about Shahaab a lot lately. We aren't paying enough attention to him. Ever since Shadi started talking so sweetly, I've forgotten all about Shahaab. I can tell from his eyes that he's upset with me and I want to make it up to him. Please let me. I'll come over every few days and take him out for a bit.'

Mother continued looking at her in a strange way. I wanted to go out with Fereshteh with all my being. What miracle had brought me this magical opportunity? I pulled on Mother's hand and looked at her with hopeful eyes. She wanted to say no, but my pleading gaze broke her resolve. She said, 'I'm not sure. I'm worried he'll cause more trouble.'

'Don't worry, he won't bother me. Will you, Shahaab?' I shook my head. 'Very good, then hurry and get ready so we can go out.'

I was mad with joy. I ran into the bathroom and washed my hands, my face and my feet, paying particular attention to my knees. Mother came and helped me. I wore my blue shorts and my blue and white chequered shirt that still smelled new. I let Mother part my hair on the side using a wet comb.

Fereshteh said, 'You look handsome. He's even prettier than Shadi isn't he?'

I took Fereshteh's hand. We walked out of the door and the sound of Shadi wailing behind us made me sort of happy and proud.

Babi said, 'Poor Shadi, she wanted to join us too.'

Asi said sternly, 'She can't! Plus, she's already been out with Mother today.'

'That doesn't count. She takes us along to do the shopping and calls it going out. She thinks we're stupid.'

This outing was different from the ones with Mother. It was as if I'd escaped from a cage. I felt light. I turned and looked at Fereshteh to see if she was as happy as I was. I wanted to thank her with my eyes, but her attention was somewhere else. She looked worried. It seemed she'd forgotten all about me even though she was holding my hand. I pulled on her hand a bit to attract her attention but she said impatiently, 'Listen, Shahaab, if you behave yourself and listen to me, I'll buy you an ice cream on the way back, okay?'

I froze. It sounded like she was bargaining. This was just like something Khosrow would say. Maybe she was planning on making fun of me too?

We crossed the street and entered the park. Fereshteh took me to the playground without a word. She seemed more nervous than before and kept looking around. I sensed that she was looking for someone. After a while, a young man walked by and whispered something. Fereshteh smiled and told me, 'Go on and play, Shahaab. I'll sit on this bench and wait for you.' She let go of my hand. I walked towards the playground but kept turning back and looking at them with curiosity. Fereshteh sat next to the stranger on the bench. It looked like they knew each other. I was beginning to grasp the reason behind Fereshteh's sudden kindness towards me. All my attention was on them. I sat on the swing for a bit, and then stood next to the slides. I spun around a pole. They didn't even look at me. I got tired and wasn't sure what else to do. I shyly walked back towards them. Fereshteh said, 'What's wrong, Shahaab? Don't you want to play any more?' I shook my head and tried to sit next to them.

The young man said, 'What if he goes and tells everyone?'

'Don't worry. He can't talk.' And then she whispered something in his ear. I hung my head. I knew they were talking about my stupidity and my lack of speech. I was more devastated than angry.

It was getting dark when Fereshteh finally said goodbye to him. She was excited all the way back and kept talking and laughing. She even gave me a kiss and bought me a delicious ice cream.

From then on these outings became part of our daily routine. Mother was happy and kept thanking Fereshteh. I enjoyed going out, playing in the park and eating ice cream, but I didn't feel any gratitude towards her. Taking me out was just an excuse for her to leave the house and meet the long-haired young man, who I now knew was called Ramin. Whenever the morality police*

* A branch of the police force in Iran responsible for preventing activities contravening Islamic law, including any contact between unrelated members of the opposite sex.

54

showed up, she would pretend to play with me, as if she was only in the park for my sake. Our relationship was really an arrangement that benefited her more than me, but we were both satisfied with it and didn't plan on changing it.

One day Fataneh came over to our house after doing her shopping, and asked Mother, 'Does Fereshteh really take Shahaab to the park every day?'

'Yes, she arrives right on the dot and takes him out. Why?'

'Nothing, I was just wondering. She's truly patient, isn't she?'

'Actually I was sort of against it myself, but she insisted.'

'That's because my daughter's so kind. She says it's good for Shahaab.'

I held my hand in front of my mouth to keep from laughing out loud.

Asi said, 'Fataneh is so dumb. She thinks Fereshteh goes to the park for our sake!'

I didn't like Ramin but I had no choice. I watched them suspiciously from behind the trees. They secretly held hands. They would lean their heads against each other when they were sure no one was there. I wanted to laugh. I didn't understand why they did these things despite such fear. Whenever the police showed up they would go pale as chalk. Ramin would walk the other way, and Fereshteh would run after me. I could even recognize the plainclothes police, and I would hurry to Fereshteh as soon as I spotted them.

One day Fereshteh and Ramin were deep in conversation, and didn't notice the police approaching. I tried to scream but my voice got stuck in my throat, just as it always did at times of stress. I ran towards them. I grabbed Fereshteh's hand and pulled with all my might. Surprised, she said, 'What are you doing?' I pointed at the police. As soon as he saw them, Ramin jumped up and started running in the opposite direction. Fereshteh and I hid behind the trees. She threw a large black shawl over her head and pulled off her colourful scarf. The police were faster than Ramin and caught up with him. One of them grabbed him by the neck and kicked his legs. Ramin fell to the ground.

We saw the whole thing from a distance. I could feel the pain in my neck and legs too. They dragged Ramin and some other people out of the park. We followed them. There were two buses outside the park: one for the boys, and the other filled with weeping girls, talking to each other and pleading with the guards at the same time. They pushed Ramin into the bus. I didn't want Fereshteh to see him in this demeaning situation. I pulled on her hand. The bus started to move and passed us. Ramin looked at Fereshteh. There was blood at the corner of his mouth. I felt sorry for him. Fereshteh kept wiping away her tears the entire way home. She didn't buy me an ice cream, but it didn't matter. She said, 'Did you see what a nice guy he is? He gave himself up so we wouldn't get into trouble. They ran after him and missed us. What will they do to him now? If they lash him, he'll die for sure.' And she burst into tears once again.

CHAPTER 14

We didn't hear from Fereshteh for a few days. Mother was surprised and kept asking, 'Why doesn't Fereshteh come to pick you up any more? Did you do something to annoy her?' I shrugged. One afternoon she showed up again. Mother said, 'I thought you were done with going to the park. Anyway, it makes sense. School will start soon and it's getting dark earlier now. It's sort of cold too. You shouldn't trouble yourself.'

Asi laughed and said, 'She's not troubling herself! She misses that boy. She'll start smiling as soon as she sees him again.'

I got ready in a flash. I was curious to see Ramin after his beating.

We ran to the park. I almost fell over laughing as soon as I saw Ramin. I had to put my hand over my mouth. Asi and Babi laughed out loud in my ears. Babi said, 'Look at him! Why did he shave his head?'

His face looked even thinner than before and he dropped his head in embarrassment. Fereshteh forgot to send me to the playground. She hurried towards Ramin and said, 'Oh my God! What have they done to you?'

'Don't look at me. I look terrible. I'm afraid you'll hate me this way.'

'Is that why you didn't want me to see you? You always look

handsome no matter what. You can't imagine how worried I was.'

Again I pressed my hand against my mouth to keep from laughing out loud. Asi and Babi were rolling on the ground laughing. I hid behind the bench.

Ramin said, 'We can't continue this way any more. They gave me a suspended sentence of forty lashes.'

'What does that mean?'

'My father begged them not to lash me, so they said if they catch me a second time, they'll give me forty lashes in addition to any new sentence.'

'Oh my God!'

'I was just thankful that you got away, otherwise who knows what would have happened.'

'But how are we going to see each other now? I'll die if I can't see you any more. I've been going crazy these past few days.'

'Me too, but it's too dangerous in the park now. We have to find a safe place to meet.'

'Like where?'

'We have to find a house. My friend Ismael has a flat. He's willing to lend me the keys so we could meet there every once in a while.'

'What? He has a flat at his age?'

'He isn't the same age as us, he's older. But he's very generous. We're good friends. He has a small market on our street. His flat is upstairs from the shop.'

'No, I'm too scared. This isn't a good idea.'

'What if they catch us on the street or the park or a restaurant? What if we get lashed? It's not like we're going to do anything improper.' Ramin suddenly jumped up and said, 'They're coming ... Same time tomorrow at the supermarket.' He rushed off.

Fereshteh and I sat on the bench for a while. I didn't feel like playing. Fereshteh looked at me and said, 'What should I do now?' I shrugged my shoulders.

Two days went by without any news from Fereshteh. I thought

our park outings were over and I wouldn't be seeing her again. But before noon on the third day our door-bell rang. It was Fereshteh. I looked at her in surprise. Mother said, 'Did your plans change? You're not going to the park in the afternoons any longer?'

'It gets really crowded in the afternoon. I thought it would be better if we went in the mornings.'

When we left the house Fereshteh said, 'Hurry up, Shahaab, it's getting late.' But we didn't walk towards the park. After running for a bit and crossing several streets, we reached a small corner market, tired and sweaty. At the owner's signal we walked to the end of the shop. There were a couple of stools and a small table placed against the wall. Fereshteh lifted me on to one of the stools and leaned against the other one and looked around. Ramin showed up. Asi said, 'He looks like a chopstick!' I laughed, and Fereshteh and Ramin looked at me in surprise. Fereshteh winked at Ramin and pointed at her head. I knew the meaning of that gesture. My face felt red. I lowered my eyes.

Fereshteh said, 'What are we going to do?'

'If they catch us here we won't have a way out. They'll shut down the shop and Ismael will get into trouble. Let's go upstairs to the flat.'

'But it's indecent for you and me to be alone in a stranger's house. What's Ismael going to think?'

'Nothing, he knows that we like each other and can't meet on the street or at a restaurant. So we don't have a choice.' He nodded towards me and continued, 'And you have a chaperone, so what are you worried about?'

It had upset me before when Fereshteh pointed at her head to show what she thought of me, but hearing these words, I grew calm and began to feel proud. An ugly man around thirty years old, with a thick moustache and curly hair, walked over to us. He handed me an ice-cream cone and said, 'Go on upstairs before you cause any trouble. If they catch you here I'll be in deep shit.'

Ramin pointed to a door and said, 'The stairs are over there, next to the toilet. I'll go first and you follow me in a few minutes.'

Fereshteh's voice shook as she said, 'Okay, we'll come as soon as Shahaab finishes his ice cream.'

'No, that'll take too long. Shahaab can stay down here and finish his ice cream until we return.'

'No. I'm not going anywhere without him.'

'Fine! Then let him bring his ice cream upstairs before I get bored.'

Ramin left. I ate some of the ice cream without any appetite. The curly-haired guy looked at us and signalled Fereshteh to go up. She was indecisive, but she finally got up and said, 'Let's get out of here, Shahaab.' I got up and she took my hand. We left the market. The guy yelled after her, but she paid no notice. We had reached the corner when we heard Ramin hurrying behind us. I tried to walk faster, but Fereshteh slowed down. Ramin reached us, out of breath. 'What happened? Why did you leave?'

'I can't do it. I don't like Ismael. He looks at me weirdly and it embarrasses me.'

'Ignore him. The poor guy has given us permission to use his flat! Don't you trust me?'

'I do trust you, but I don't like that place.'

'So what are we going to do? Do you know of another place we could go? Or do you want to break up and stop seeing me?'

'No, no . . . I can't stand being away from you.'

'Me too. I'll go crazy if I don't see you. We can't meet on the street, so we don't have a choice. I have a lot to tell you. You can't imagine the things that have happened to me. The police became suspicious about our phone calls too. How long has it been since we've really talked? Just come over there this once, and if you don't like it, we won't go again.'

Fereshteh squeezed my hand and with hesitant steps walked back towards the market. This time we went straight to the rear of the shop. The stairs were dark and smelled bad. I pinched my nose. We went through a dark door at the top of the stairs and entered a large room. It was messy and dirty, and smelled of stale cigarette smoke. Clothes were strewn all over the furniture. There was a pillow and some bunched-up sheets on a sofa, dirty dishes on the table and large overflowing ashtrays here and there. An ugly plastic skeleton and a few awful paintings were hanging on the walls. There was a flower-pot with dead flowers on the TV. I hated everything about the room and missed our own clean, bright house. Fereshteh frowned and said, 'Why does it look like this?'

'It's a bachelor pad. What did you expect? He doesn't have anyone, and he works all day and doesn't have time to clean up.'

I noticed Ramin was still holding my melting ice-cream cone. He placed it in front of me, turned on the TV and said, 'Be a good boy, watch some TV and finish your ice cream.' They sat right behind me on the sofa. At first they talked about the police, the court, their worries and other stuff, but then their voices grew quiet and I couldn't make out what they were saying any more. When they stopped talking I turned around and looked at them. Fereshteh had taken off her scarf and coat and had her head on Ramin's shoulder. They were holding hands and Ramin was sniffing her hair with excitement. With all my heart, I wished we were sitting in the park instead.

The same thing happened the following day. This time Ramin put a video in the VCR and turned up the volume. 'This is a great movie, Shahaab.'

I looked at them suspiciously. I sat in front of the TV and tried to listen to what they were saying, but they didn't make a sound. I turned around. Oh my God! I automatically placed my hand on my mouth and turned back, but all my attention was on them. I don't know why Fereshteh suddenly got off the sofa. I stood up too. I grabbed her hand and pulled her to the door.

Ramin pleaded with her, 'What's wrong? What happened? I didn't mean it. I love you. I need you.'

'I know. That's why I don't want to meet you here any more.'

'I swear I won't do it again.'

'It's better if we meet in the park. I have to go. Goodbye, see you tomorrow at the park.'

I was proud of Fereshteh. I took her hand and we went down

the stairs. Fereshteh let me lead her. The air outside was clean and I took a deep breath.

The next day we went to the park just like before. Fereshteh took me to the playground and looked around anxiously. Ramin was behind the trees observing us from afar. He signalled to Fereshteh not to look at him. She was confused. I didn't have fun playing in the playground. I got off the swing and took Fereshteh's hand. We slowly walked back home.

With each passing day Fereshteh seemed sadder and lonelier, until one day when the guards were busy with more important things, Fereshteh and Ramin had the chance to sit together in the park and talk for a while. Their eyes shone with happiness and I was happy too. Whenever they were together in the park, I felt a sense of comfort. On the way back Fereshteh talked to me happily, and told me her dreams and secrets. I listened to her carefully. I knew that she didn't expect me to answer and just wanted to be heard. In the end she said, 'I can't stop seeing him, Shahaab! I wish it were safe to meet in the park! Can you watch out for us and let us know whenever the police come?' I nodded. I felt proud and was willing to do anything for her as long as they didn't return to that disgusting room.

The following day the park still felt safe. I circled their bench like a security guard keeping a lookout. A few teenagers ran past me looking scared. I became afraid, and like a detective in a movie hid behind a tree. The police entered from a street at the top and suddenly spread all over the park. I ran as fast as I could and reached Fereshteh. They jumped up as soon as they saw my scared face.

Ramin said, 'Are they here?' He ran behind a tree but was captured by a guard who had been hiding there the entire time.

Another one showed up behind Fereshteh and said in an angry voice, 'Hurry up, let's go!' The two of them were white as chalk. I think I probably looked the same.

Fereshteh said in a shaking voice, 'I swear we weren't doing anything!'

'Get going!'

They led us, trembling with fear, to the park's entrance. Ramin's lips looked blue as he said, 'Let them go. It was all my fault.'

'Shut up! We'll be taking in all of you for now.'

The guard pushed Ramin to make him go faster. Ramin tripped and fell over. He stood up again, humiliated. Fereshteh was crying and I looked away so I wouldn't see him so ashamed. His humiliation embarrassed me. At the park entrance they handed Fereshteh over to the transport for women, which had two female guards. Fereshteh thought the women would be more understanding, and she started to plead and cry more. But it seemed they were even harsher than the men. They pushed her into the bus. I was about to faint with fear. I held on to Fereshteh's dress, screaming in terror. The officer in charge, who was a middle-aged man, came forwards. Fereshteh pleaded with him, 'Please sir, I haven't done anything. This child is dumb and can't speak. I brought him to the park and now he's having a heart attack. Please let me take him home!'

The woman in charge of the bus said, 'Get back in!' She turned to the officer in charge and said, 'She's lying. I know her type. Leave her to me.' I screamed even more without knowing how I was doing it. The guards looked at us with uncertainty.

Fereshteh jumped out of the bus and said, 'He's going to faint! He's epileptic too.'

The man in charge said, 'Take him home.'

'No sir! It's all an act. Look at her hijab! I'll quieten the kid myself. Just let me—'

'Zahra, let her go. You, go ahead and leave, but don't let me catch you here again.'

Fereshteh grabbed my hand and we both ran towards home, crying the entire way. When we got there, Fereshteh said, 'We'll go to my house first. My mother isn't in. We'll clean you up and then I'll take you to your house.'

Fereshteh took out her keys and quietly opened the door. There was no one in. She fell on her bed upstairs and began to cry. I sat on the floor and leaned my head against the wall. I was too tired to move. We both grew calmer after a few minutes. Fereshteh was sitting on the bed and said, 'Did you see how they beat up poor Ramin? What about the lashes they'll give him? Oh my God! He won't be able to take it. He will surely die!' She started crying once again. I went towards her. I felt sorry for her. I caressed her hair. She hugged me and said, 'What are we going to do now? Should we let his parents know so they can go after him?' She stretched out her hand, picked up the phone and dialled a number. After a few moments, trying to make her voice sound older, she said, 'The guards arrested your son Ramin in the park today. You should go and help him out,' and she hung up.

The park excursions were put on hold for a while. Fereshteh was depressed and nervous, always getting into an argument at home. She would come over to our house and cry over different things. Fataneh had had it with her. One day she told Mother, 'I don't know what's got into her. She's always complaining. She's in a bad mood all the time. Does she say anything when she comes over here?'

'Not really. She just says that Khosrow bothers her and that she's upset. Then she goes to Shahaab's room.'

'Rubbish! Poor Khosrow. He's no angel, but he's not as bad as she claims either.'

After ten days Fereshteh showed up happy and excited again, wearing a colourful scarf and some make-up. She said, 'Get up, Shahaab! We haven't been out in a long time.' Mother looked at her thoughtfully. 'You're going to the park again?'

'I'm bored. School will start in a few days and I won't be able to take Shahaab out any more. We should take advantage of these few remaining days.'

A thousand questions went through my mind. What's happened now? Is Ramin out? Aren't they scared to go to the park again? If I see the guards one more time I'll faint.

As soon as the door shut behind us and I was alone with Fereshteh, I stood still, pulled at her hand and stared at her. Fereshteh stared back and said, 'What? Let's go. Are you afraid?' I nodded. 'Don't be scared. We're not going to the park. We're going to the market to see Ramin and then we'll come right back. That's all.' I screwed up my face in disgust and shook my head. 'What can I do? We don't have anywhere else to meet. I don't have a choice. I'm going mad. I miss him so much. Don't you miss him at all?' I shook my head again. She laughed and said, 'That's because you don't love him. You don't even know what love is. I've been thinking about him all this time. He's a wonderful guy. He's been thinking about me too. I was so worried for him. Do you know how many lashes they gave him? Poor boy! It was all my fault. This is the first day he's been able to leave home. I have to see him. He said the doctors have told him that his kidneys may fail because of the lashes he received! If I hadn't made a fuss and had kept going to Ismael's room none of this would have happened.'

Asi said, 'What a disaster! From now on we'll always have to go there.'

That day Fereshteh and Ramin were very happy. Ramin proudly showed her his scars. Fereshteh looked at him with worry and asked, 'Does it hurt?' He heroically told her everything that had happened and she praised his bravery.

Fereshteh gradually got used to meeting him in that disgusting room, but I got bored there. I disliked Ismael who wanted me to sit on his lap. I hated that Fereshteh and Ramin were always glued together. One day Ramin said, 'Shahaab, go downstairs and get us a drink.' I didn't like going downstairs by myself. I was afraid of Ismael. I ignored him and turned around. Ramin took my hand and said, 'Go on, be a good boy. He's put aside a special ice cream for you too. My scars still hurt. Go and get us something. I'm dying of thirst.' I looked at Fereshteh who was sitting silently. I couldn't understand anything from her eyes.

I went downstairs scared. I pointed at the drinks. With a hideous smile, Ismael handed me a bottle and two glasses. After a couple of steps I noticed that he was following me. I dropped the bottle out of fear and ran to the stairs. His ugly face looked even scarier in the dark staircase. He was about to catch me when the bells above the door announced a new customer. Ismael returned to the market. I went upstairs with shaking legs. I pulled the door handle but it was locked. I kicked at the door. I was getting very upset. I sat behind the door and started to cry.

Babi said, 'We are a miserable creature. They can do whatever they want to us because we can't talk. No one is concerned about us.'

I was upset with Fereshteh for allowing Ramin to do this to me, and now she wouldn't even open the door. After a few minutes she opened the door holding her scarf and overcoat, and arguing with Ramin. Her hair was dishevelled. She put on her scarf in the stairwell and wore her coat in the market. I ran out of the door ahead of her. I cried the entire way back home and her caresses didn't calm me down. I didn't trust her any longer. Inside I felt betrayed by her and decided never to go out with her again. I would hide whenever she came round, and once when she tried to force me to go out with her I screamed, held on to the banister and cried. Mother was surprised by my reaction, but she helped me anyway.

Fereshteh left and my summer entertainment came to an end. I had learned a lot during this time, things that were too advanced for my age. My mind was preoccupied. I couldn't fully understand much of what had happened. Sometimes Asi, Babi and I would talk about it in embarrassment. I tried acting it out with Shadi once, but yuck! It felt disgusting. I told Asi, 'Ugh, her mouth is full of spit!'

CHAPTER 15

The kids started school again and our lives resumed their old routine. Fereshteh didn't come back to see Shahaab again. I don't know what happened between them, but Shahaab didn't want to go out with her any more. He had grown quieter and more introverted, and didn't even run around the room playing his strange games. He no longer showed me the drawings he made, and the few times I accidentally saw them I couldn't make head nor tail of the jumbled lines. Once when he saw me looking at one he grabbed it and tore it up, and I sensed it was something I shouldn't have seen. My main worry however was his relationship with his father. Nasser was a decent, hard-working man who had dedicated his life to his family, but he lacked something; something he should have learned as a child. He didn't know how to show his love. He found the expression of emotions ridiculous, and felt ashamed to do so. He thought anything that wasn't based on pure logic was pointless and unnecessary. He was a perfectionist and didn't forgive any shortcomings in me, or our children. Arash tried so hard to meet his father's demands that he too became obsessive in this regard. He buried himself in schoolwork and private tutors. Nasser spoke of him with pride and everyone applauded his efforts, and this made him obsess about school more and more. Once Nasser became convinced that Shahaab was mentally deficient, his expectations of Arash grew even more. It was as if the only way he could put up with the shame of having a dumb child was to have his other son be a genius.

How could such a person understand Shahaab? They did not have a healthy emotional bond and grew further apart day by day, and I was worried and confused, trying all sorts of tricks to create a connection between them. One day I handed a plate of fruit to Shahaab and asked him to take it to his father. He slammed the plate on the table.

'Shahaab, what's wrong? Your dad just got home and he's tired. Take him some fruit and sit next to him. He misses you.'

He didn't look pleased. I handed him the plate once again.

'Go on, son, don't be so stubborn. Take this to your father. Don't you love him?'

He pressed his lips together and threw the plate. It broke into pieces.

Nasser yelled, 'What was that?'

I looked at Shahaab in confusion. He ran and hid in his room.

'Nothing . . . I dropped a plate.'

CHAPTER 16

Mother pissed me off every time she talked about Father. Asi said, 'She's such an idiot! He isn't our father; he's Arash's father. Mother can speak, and is so smart she can tell whenever we want something, so why can't she understand this simple fact? Doesn't she know that good, normal, clever, pretty children belong to fathers, and dumb, ugly, sick kids who can't talk belong to mothers? If she just paid a bit of attention to Arash's father she would understand. But her mind is always somewhere else. She's always worrying about us. She doesn't notice that when Arash's father calls him, he always says, "Come here, son", and proudly introduces Arash as his son wherever he goes. When he looks at him his eyes fill with kindness and laughter. But he doesn't like looking at us at all. He doesn't like showing us to other people. He always tells Mother, "Come and get your kid," meaning this one is your son, not mine. Why doesn't she understand these things? We don't need him anyway, Mother is enough for us.'

I really don't know where and when Father and I became so cut off from each other. My first memory of our detachment is from the day they brought Shadi home. Father was lovingly holding her in his arms. His eyes shone. Back then I used to go to him as soon as he got home. I'd get to the door and lift up my arms so he would pick me up. The nicest, highest place for seeing the world was up there in his arms. He would say, 'Now, give me a kiss,' and I would happily obey. Father had still not given up on talking to me, and didn't know that I was retarded. But on that particular day he didn't pick me up no matter how long I kept my arms up circling around him. He didn't even notice me. He finally kissed Shadi and put her in her cot. When I tried to kiss her too in order to gain his attention, he pushed me aside. I stood next to him feeling hopeless and alone. Shadi started to cry. Father jumped up to get Mother, and stepped on my small feet. I screamed out in pain but he'd gone to bring Shadi's bottle. When he returned he gave me a cold look and said, 'Why are you screaming?' He hadn't even noticed he'd stepped on my foot. The next day Mother asked, 'Why is his foot bruised?' and Father who had stayed at home to help out for a few days said, 'Who knows? Maybe he hit it somewhere.'

This lack of attention at that particularly sensitive time showed me I didn't have a place in my father's heart. I began to stay away from him, afraid that he would step on me again. After he came home a couple of times and forgot to pick me up, not noticing my raised arms, I sat in front of the mirror on the wardrobe door, looked at myself, tiny and helpless, and promised I would never greet him with happy kisses again.

The longer it took me to begin talking, the more distant Father became. It was as if my presence was an insult to his character, offending his pride and manhood. He would look at me in confusion, wondering why God had granted him such a son. He never spoke to me again. He probably thought talking to someone who couldn't respond was ridiculous. I'm not saying he did all this on purpose, but he was embarrassed by my presence, and I understood this despite my age.

I remember the first time they took me to a speech specialist. The room was dark and everything in it was brown. There was a scary picture hanging on the wall that looked like a butterfly drawn by a crazy person. Shadi was eighteen months old and could say many words. Her every childish utterance was like a slap on my face. Everyone looked at me questioningly, wondering, 'Why can't you talk? She's younger than you and she speaks.'

The issue of talking gradually became a source of constant anxiety for me. Every time I needed to say something my heart would beat like mad, I would hear a whistling sound, and the voices around me would grow dim and hard to understand.

My father told the doctor, 'He's almost four years old and can't talk yet. His eighteen-month-old sister can talk up a storm.'

Mother automatically said, 'Knock on wood,' and rapped on the doctor's desk.

Father continued, 'His doctor says there's nothing wrong with him, that he'll start sooner or later, but I think it's getting too late. Maybe we should be doing something.'

'Does he have any other problems?'

Mother said, 'He recently started to wet himself again even though he stopped doing that a long time ago.'

I looked at her, startled. I couldn't believe she would embarrass me like this in front of a stranger. It had only happened twice and it was all her fault anyway. She hadn't paid attention and had taken her time getting to me, so what shouldn't have happened had happened.

'Children usually do that for attention. Do you pay enough attention to him?'

Father said, 'We do everything we can for him. But it seems he has a problem in this area too. He is very cold and unemotional. He never seems happy to see me, even when I've been away for a long time. He tries to get away every time I try to embrace him. He won't let me kiss him and doesn't acknowledge any kindness. I buy him toys but they don't make him happy even for a moment. He doesn't look at them at all.'

Mother said, 'That's not true. He plays with them when you're not around. He just doesn't notice them at first – it's as if he doesn't recognize them as something new. Sometimes I think he's just being stubborn.'

Father said, 'But why? A kid this age doesn't know what being stubborn is.'

71

The doctor asked, 'Does he have any physical problems? Did he start walking on time? Can he hear well?'

Mother answered, 'I'm not sure. Shadi began walking two weeks before her first birthday, but he started when he was fifteen months old. I don't know about his hearing. The doctor examined him and said his hearing was okay, and he understands when I talk to him. But sometimes when he's watching a cartoon or playing, he doesn't hear me when I call. He has these strange games he plays. He runs around the pool for hours looking up at the sky and then he suddenly stops, and after a moment starts running again. It looks crazy! It makes me dizzy but he won't listen when I tell him to stop.'

The doctor stepped forwards, 'Put him on the bed.'

I didn't like doctors. They were unpredictable. Sometimes they would give you sweets, and other times they would poke you with a needle for no reason, claiming it wouldn't hurt at all! That statement pissed me off even more than the needle itself. It made me want to stick a needle in them just to see if it hurt or not. My own doctor had nice white hair. He was kind and small. But with his thick, dark moustache and massive size, this doctor reminded me of a cartoon villain. He wasn't likeable at all. Especially since he discussed all my shortcomings with my parents in front of me, and made them compare me to Shadi and her achievements. Father lifted me off the floor. I didn't like sitting on examination beds. I stiffened my legs so he wouldn't be able to sit me down. With a severe glance Father forced me to sit.

He told the doctor, 'See! I don't understand why he's so obstinate sometimes.' The doctor didn't answer him and began to examine my ears, throat, my heart and stomach. The stethoscope was cold and made me shiver.

'Sit still!' He lifted the stethoscope and brought his face close to mine and said, 'You can hear me, can't you?'

I looked at his black moustache. Two of the hairs sticking out of his nose had turned white. Babi said, 'It looks like snot!' I wanted to laugh. The doctor kept talking but all my attention was on his moustache that moved up and down in a silly way. I thought maybe it wasn't white hair after all and was really snot coming out of his nose. I turned my face away.

The doctor called my name and turned my face around again and said, 'Look at me.'

I forcefully turned my face away. Babi said, 'Ugh ... why doesn't he clean his nose? That's disgusting!'

'Look here, son.' He turned my face again. 'Clap, like this.' He clapped his hands together making a loud noise. 'Let me see you clap.'

I looked at him with bitterness. Babi said, 'Idiot! He thinks we're Shadi's age and need to play clapping games!' I felt insulted. I crossed my arms and turned my head away.

The doctor was getting angry. From the waiting room we could hear the sound of children crying and arguing. The receptionist stuck her head in and said, 'Doctor they're making a racket in the waiting room. There are still a lot of patients waiting. And you won't get to—'

The doctor pointed her to her desk, turned round to me and sternly said, 'Did you understand what I asked you to do? Clap your hands together.' I turned my head away and pressed my crossed arms tightly to my chest.

The doctor was clearly upset. He easily uncrossed my arms. The effort it took to force my arms together, the doctor's assault on my personal space and his eventual victory over me, made me turn red. I had to defend myself. I bent my head towards the doctor's hand that was holding mine tightly, and with my small sharp teeth bit him hard.

The doctor said, 'Ouch!' and let go of my hands. I had to run away. Even though the bed was tall, I jumped off and ran into the other room. My parents looked on in shock. Father got up to follow me, but the doctor said, 'Let him go, it's not important. It's not just a speech problem. I think he has mental problems as well. We have to run some tests. It will be a bit costly. You can ask the receptionist for more information. Call to make an appointment whenever you've made up your minds.' And he opened the door like he couldn't wait to get rid of us. Mother picked Shadi up in a hurry, grabbed her handbag and left the room. Father reached me with a few steps. He picked me up and we left.

They didn't take me back for the tests. Mother was against it from the start. She said, 'This doctor doesn't know anything. Dr Tabatabayi is right – he said there was nothing wrong with him, that he'll start talking on his own at some point.' And Father changed his mind when he found out the cost of the tests. But now he was convinced I had a mental problem which caused my lack of speech. He kept his opinion to himself, of course, because he didn't want to witness Mother's painful reaction. Eventually, in order to make a final decision about my mental health, he decided to try one last time to somehow force me to speak, or give his final verdict on the issue of whether I was retarded once and for all.

My troubles became tenfold from then on. Father would get home from work tired. He would wash and then call me. He tried to be calm and cheery, but it was obvious he hated the responsibility he'd taken upon himself. With false patience he would sit me down next to him and say, 'Shahaab, say, "apple", "apple"!' I would press my lips together and stare at the floor, ready to make a run for it at the first chance. Father would repeat, 'Go like this and say, "Aa".' His voice would begin to tremble, showing his internal stress, and it would scare me more and more. Then the arguments would start, 'It's easy, just say, "apple"! Do you understand me?'

I would become completely tongue-tied. My heart racing, I would press my lips together, too hurt to talk to this man. Shadi would finally free herself from wherever Mother was keeping her, and run to us. Or maybe Mother would let her go on purpose so she would come and save me. Laughing, she would dig her way into Father's arms without any embarrassment. His face would break into a smile and he would tell Mum, who had come to take Shadi away, 'Let her stay, she's not bothering me.' Then he would hug her and kiss her head. I didn't like watching this scene at all.

After that the lesson would change. But Father still wouldn't give up; he'd continue, 'Say, "apple".'

Then Shadi would proudly yell, 'Apple!' If she hadn't been in his arms, I would have smacked her on the head.

'Just make a sound so I know you have a voice. What does a cat say?'

And with her high-pitched voice Shadi would go, 'Meow!' She would continue showing off and Father would become more and more absorbed in her, forgetting about me, and giving me a chance to escape and hide in my room. After a while, Father left me to myself and our miserable lessons came to an end.

CHAPTER 17

It was late autumn. Fereshteh came over at around four in the afternoon. She looked thinner and pale. I ran up the stairs but sat next to the banister to hear her talking. Fereshteh asked Mother, 'Tell Shahaab to come down. I want to take him out.' Mother looked at her, surprised, and said, 'What's going on again? Why do you want to take him out? School has started and I've heard you have a lot of homework. It's cold outside and gets dark earlier. I don't think these outings are such a good idea any more.'

'I just want to relax a bit at the park. I'll take my books and study while Shahaab plays. I get bored in the house. I can study better outside in the fresh air.'

Asi said, 'What a liar! Don't go with her!'

Mother said, 'I'm not sure. What you do is up to you and your parents. But I don't think Shahaab really wants to go.'

'Can I ask him myself?'

I ran to my room, hid under the covers and pretended to be asleep. Fereshteh walked in. She sat next to the bed and said in a quiet voice, 'Get up! Stop being a brat. It's not nap time. Let's go to the park.' I turned my back to her. 'I promise we'll just go to the park. Ramin really wants to see you. He's bought you a really cool car. Come on! I'm late.'

Her sudden silence made me curious. I peeked from under the covers. She had turned even paler and was looking at Mother standing by the door. We weren't sure how long she had been there and what she had heard. Fereshteh stuttered, 'He's pretending to be asleep.'

Mother looked at her suspiciously and said, 'Let him be. You know how stubborn he is. He'll never do something he doesn't want to. He'll just give you a hard time if you force him to go. If you're bored at home just stay and study here.'

Asi laughed and said, 'Mother's so stupid!' We stuck our head under the covers and laughed.

Fereshteh got up sadly, patted my back through the covers and said, 'So you're going to leave me in suspense too . . . ' Then she left.

It was getting dark when someone rang the door-bell. Mother pressed the buzzer and opened the door. Khosrow ran into the hall. As soon as he saw me he said, 'Oh! So you're back? Where's Fereshteh? Why won't she come home?' He yelled, 'Fereshteh! Where are you? Hurry up! Father will be home soon.'

Mother stepped forwards and said, 'Khosrow, what's going on? Are you looking for Fereshteh?'

'Oh, hi! Yes. Why is she hanging out here? Tell her to come home.'

'Fereshteh isn't here.'

'So how did Shahaab get back home? Wasn't he with her?'

'No. Fereshteh came over this afternoon to take him out, but he didn't go. Isn't she back yet?'

'Then who did she go with?'

'Maybe she went by herself. She wanted to go to the park to study.'

Khosrow ran out of the house without saying goodbye. Five minutes later he reappeared with Fataneh.

'Maryam, where is Fereshteh?'

'I don't know. She came here this afternoon to pick up Shahaab, but he wasn't feeling well and didn't join her. I thought she returned home.'

'No, she didn't! What am I going to do? There'll be trouble if her father finds out.'

'It's not that late. She had her books with her. She wanted to study.'

Fataneh replied with frustration, 'It's cold and dark outside! What a liar. Like Hassani, who would only go to school on Saturdays!'*

'Maybe she's gone to study with a friend.'

'What friend?'

'How should I know? You know her friends. Don't you have their numbers? Call them and see if she's there?'

'At this time of night?'

'Young people never notice the time when they get together.'

Khosrow said, 'She's probably gone over to Sousan's again. Her number's in the phonebook. Let's call her.'

'Okay. Sorry to bother you, Maryam. Please don't tell Nasser. Thank God his mother moved back home, otherwise she would leak it to him. She'll probably show up soon wherever she is.'

'Let me know when she gets back.'

'Okay.'

Mother turned to me as soon as they left. 'I'm glad you didn't go with her. Why didn't you want to go? Do you know where she is?' I shrugged.

An hour later Father and Arash got home. Poor Arash was so tired he could hardly walk. Mother ran up to him and helped him with his backpack and said, 'Go and wash. Supper is ready. You're very tired, aren't you?'

Arash kept nodding off over supper. Mother said, 'Arash, eat your food and go to bed.'

'I can't. I have to study for a test tomorrow.'

'No, darling. Go to bed. You're too tired to study now. I'll wake you up early tomorrow.'

Arash had a few more mouthfuls and dragged himself off to

* A Persian saying about the pointlessness of doing things at the wrong time.

78

his room. Mother asked Father, 'Why do you pressure him so much? Why did he need an extra maths class? He's doing pretty well in school.'

'No, he's not! He got a B in maths.'

'That's a good grade at his level. He's not in junior school any more. His subjects are more difficult now. He can't always earn an A.'

'Of course he can! My son has to participate in the mathematical Olympiad. If we don't tend to him now he'll never earn first prize.'

'So what? His health is more important than any prize! Why do you care so much about him winning first prize anyway?'

'I'm concerned about his future. This one has to be our pride and joy.'

'So that's it! His future is just an excuse. You're only thinking about yourself. You want to show off and tell everyone that he's first in his class. You don't care if he breaks under all this pressure.'

She angrily picked up the dishes and put them in the sink.

Asi said, 'Good for her! Mother is really clever sometimes.'

I was brushing my teeth when the door-bell went. Father picked up the intercom receiver and listened to the caller. He said, 'It's my brother! What's he doing here at this time of night?' He opened the door he'd just locked. My uncle, Khosrow and Fataneh all stepped in. Father said, 'What's going on?'

'I'm ruined! Fereshteh is missing!'

Mother asked Fataneh, 'She wasn't at her friend's? Did you call?'

'Yes, we called all the numbers in her address book. No one knows where she is!'

Father asked, 'Didn't she say where she was going? She just left without asking permission? When did she go?'

'I don't know! Ask her mother!'

Fataneh burst into tears. 'She went to take Shahaab out like she usually does. My poor girl is so kind, she wanted to do something for this child. She thought she could make him talk. Since the beginning of the summer she's spent several hours each day trying to teach him things. I kept asking her to stop, to pay more attention to her own schoolwork. I told her it was a waste of time. But she felt sorry for him. She said someone had to do something. She wanted to make her uncle happy. Today when she came to pick him up Shahaab didn't go with her. I don't know where she went!'

Mother was surprised and replied angrily, 'What do you mean, every day? It's been more than three months since Shahaab went out with her!'

'What? She didn't take Shahaab to the park? I came and asked you once myself!'

'That was during the summer. She came and took him to the park for a month, or a month and a half. But then Shahaab didn't want to go any more, so she didn't come back until this afternoon. But Shahaab didn't want to go this time either.'

Uncle, Fataneh and Khosrow stared at Mother in confusion. My uncle grasped the situation before the rest and his anger became tenfold. He turned to Fataneh and said, 'So where has she been going every afternoon?' Fataneh began to stutter. She turned pale and said, 'I really don't know! Maryam, are you sure? Maybe she picked him up on the street and you didn't notice.'

Mother was clearly angry now. 'What are you saying? Since when have my children been out on the streets without my knowing? I check on them every five minutes. How can he be gone for two hours without my noticing? No! Wherever she went, she went on her own, not with my son.'

Uncle yelled at Fataneh, 'It's all your fault, woman! The way you've raised your kids, each one worse than the other! What kind of a mother are you? Your daughter was out two hours every day and you never knew where she was?'

'What do you expect from me? She's not just *my* child! Why didn't you pay any attention yourself? My poor daughter wanted to help your nephew. Did you expect me to say no?'

'Haven't you understood yet that it was just an excuse?'

80

Father stepped in and said, 'This is not the time to argue. The important issue now is to find Fereshteh. Do you have any idea where she may be?'

'I've called all her friends and she's not with any of them.'

'What about family? Maybe she's at her grandmother's?'

Fataneh said, 'No! If they find out it'll be terrible. Maryam, please keep this to yourself. Don't let anyone know.'

'Don't worry. I never see anyone anyway, and I don't spend an hour each day on the phone with my in-laws, giving them a report on everything that's going on!'

Fataneh was perturbed. Father said, 'She would go to one of the relatives if she were upset. Did you two have an argument? Was she upset before she left?'

'No, we didn't have an argument. I just told her to leave this child alone. I said if he were improvable, he'd have improved by now. She didn't answer me. She hasn't been herself lately. She's more introverted and has lost weight. She's depressed. I thought it was because she was worried about Shahaab.' Mother smirked.

Uncle said, 'I think we should call Mother. We don't need to say anything. We'll know from her tone if something's going on.'

Fataneh said, 'I talked to her for an hour this afternoon. She'll get suspicious if I call again. Maybe Maryam should call her.'

'Me? She'll be more suspicious if I call, because I only ring her if I have something important to say.'

Father said, 'Do you want me to phone just to see how she is?'

Uncle said, 'Yes, Nasser, you call. She'll tell you if she knows anything.'

Father picked up the phone and talked to Grandmother and Aunt Shahin. Fataneh called her sisters too but it was useless. Fataneh began to cry. Uncle kept pacing the living room worriedly. I was confused. Asi and Babi were silent too. Father said, 'We should call the police.'

Fataneh said, 'Oh no!'

Mother suddenly jumped up as if she'd found a solution, 'I know! They've probably taken her in.'

'Who's taken her?'

'The morality police! Don't worry. It's not a big deal. These days they constantly arrest young boys and girls in the park.'

'What for?'

'For different things. The most basic is improper hijab.'

Father said, 'Maryam's right. She probably went to the park after she left here. Haven't you seen how they collect teenagers every hour and take them to the station?'

Uncle said angrily, 'That shameless girl! I'll let her have it! How was she dressed?'

Mother tried to calm him down; 'You don't have to be dressed improperly for the morality police to find fault.'

'So, what now?'

Father said, 'Nothing. We'll check out the stations and find her.'

'I'll kill her.'

'Calm down, brother. Let's find her first.'

Mother said, 'Hossein, don't disturb yourself. These days every parent with a teenager has had their child arrested by the morality police. When I still worked at the office my co-workers each had stories about their kids and how they'd been picked up by the morality police. These things are pretty common now. Don't take it too hard. You should count your blessings if you find her there, it could be a lot worse.' Everyone stared at Mother like they were each imagining something awful.

They sent Khosrow home so he could let everyone know if Fereshteh returned, or if there were a phone call. Father and Uncle left in the car to go and check different police stations. Fataneh stayed with Mother to keep from going crazy with worry. Shadi had fallen asleep on the sofa without anyone noticing. Mother picked her up and came upstairs. I ran into my room and pretended to be asleep. Mother placed Shadi in her bed, and then sat on mine. She took off my socks and pulled the sheets over me. She caressed my head and kissed me softly on the cheek. I loved it when she did this.

CHAPTER 18

I woke up in the middle of the night at the sound of the door-bell and voices talking. I'm not sure if I'd slept at all. I went to the top of the stairs. Mother and Fataneh were questioning Father and Uncle.

'What happened? Did you find her?'

I was sitting in the dark, leaning against the banister. Uncle was hunched over and Father helped him to the sofa. Fataneh pulled at her hair and wept. 'What's happened to him?'

'Nothing, his back seized up again. We couldn't find her.'

Mother asked anxiously, 'She wasn't there? Where did you go?'

'Everywhere. We went to all the police stations. We even checked all the hospitals around here. We had to inform the police. No one knows anything. We're going to the morgue in the morning.'

Fataneh screamed and fainted on the sofa.

Mother said, 'Watch what you're saying in front of the poor woman!'

It seemed like that difficult night was never going to end. They spread a blanket on the floor so Uncle could lie down on a hard surface. He lay down staring at the ceiling. The rest of them sat on the sofa. Fataneh wept constantly. I stood up and went back into my room.

I woke up from a nightmare early the next day, covered in

sweat. Shadi was still asleep. It was quiet everywhere. I walked out of the room and gently pushed open the door to my parents' bedroom. They hadn't slept in their bed. I was afraid they might have left the house. I quietly crept down the stairs. I calmed down when I saw Father asleep on the sofa. I went into the kitchen looking for Mother but she wasn't there. A pale light shone from under Arash's door. I stuck my head into the room. He was sitting behind his desk studying. Mother was lying down on his bed. I slowly walked inside and stood by the bed. Mum was surprised to see me. 'Why are you up so early? It's only six-thirty! You slept really late last night.' I lay down beside her and pressed myself to her. I felt safe next to her. Arash turned around and asked, 'Was he up when Uncle came over?'

'Yes, I didn't notice what time he fell asleep.'

'So all that "concern" for Shahaab was a lie?'

Mother said, 'I was suspicious from the start.'

'Then why did you let her take Shahaab to the park?'

'Because Fereshteh is different from the rest of them. She's a sweet girl. When Shahaab was little she really liked him.'

'Yes, but once Shadi arrived she dumped him. So what'll happen now? Will they find her?'

'God knows. And even if they do, who knows what state she'll be in. We can only pray. Poor Fataneh, may God help her.'

'Is Dad going to take me to school today?'

'No, darling. Let him sleep a bit. He was up all night and has to pick up your uncle at eight. They have a tough day ahead of them.'

'Okay, I'll go to school on my own. I have an English class in the afternoon so he doesn't have to pick me up either. I'll come home afterwards.'

'Skip your afternoon class. I don't like you coming home by yourself in the evening.'

'I'm not a girl. No one's going to kidnap me!'

'I know, but just skip it this once! It won't be the end of the world.'

'I'd love to, but I'm afraid Dad will give me a hard time if I don't go.'

84

'I'll deal with him. Just hurry back home. We may need your help here.'

I couldn't have any breakfast. I felt sick. What had become of Fereshteh? Had Ramin done anything to her? What did they do in that room anyway? I wish they'd never gone into that disgusting flat. Why didn't the guards let them go to the park? They behaved well in the park and never did anything bad. They just talked.

Fataneh came over to our place after Father and Uncle had left. She was still crying. Mother tried to console her but it was clear she didn't even believe what she said herself. Mother brought the breakfast tray into the hall. She sat Shadi down in front of her and fed her. Fataneh said, 'Who can I talk to about what's happened to us? What a disgrace! What misery! What have I done to deserve this?'

Mother tried again to calm her down with hopeful words. For the first time they acted like two friends. Neither of them wanted to prove her superiority to the other. They didn't exchange verbal jibes. They were both truly distressed and sad. I felt sorry for Fataneh. Shadi was ignoring breakfast and was playing. Mother was talking to Fataneh and had forgotten all about the toast and jam in her hand. Fataneh said, 'So she was lying every time she said she was going to the park? When did Shahaab stop going with her?'

'A long time ago. I think it was in August. They came back one day and I could tell Shahaab had been crying. When Fereshteh came to pick him up the next day he even refused to come down to see her. She promised him ice cream and toys, but it didn't do any good. I was a bit surprised by Fereshteh's insistence.'

'What do you think had happened?'

'I asked Fereshteh. She said Shahaab was playing on the swings and she was sitting on the ground next to him, but then saw a few of her friends. She went with them to buy something from the food stand. When Shahaab noticed she'd gone he became upset. He thought she had left him and so wouldn't go out with her any more.'

'That sounds about right.'

'I don't know. Shahaab's always been sensitive about being left alone. Back when I used to go to work he would cry every day when I left, as if it were the first time he had been left alone. I think he's always afraid we'll leave him alone. Whenever we go out he holds my hand tightly, like he's afraid I'll run away! But his anger towards Fereshteh continued for a long time. I think it had to have another reason.'

'I wish he could talk. I wish he were different.'

Mother got upset. 'Different how?'

'I'm sorry! Please don't be upset. I can't help myself. I don't feel well at all. Please don't be upset with me. You're my only support now. I just meant it would be great if he could speak. Maybe he knows something that could help us.'

'Hang on! You give Shadi her breakfast and I'll go and talk to him.'

I was sitting on the bottom step all this time, listening to them.

Asi said, 'What should we do? Should we tell them? Should we take them to the small market?'

Babi said, 'No! Do you remember how she was afraid someone would find out about the place? What if we tell them and Uncle finds out? She said if he found out he would kill her.'

Asi continued, 'And Ismael! What if he hugs us and runs after us again? I hate him so much.'

Mother walked towards the steps. I ran upstairs, went into my room and hid under the covers of my rumpled bed, which she hadn't had time to make that day. She gently pulled the covers off me and said, 'Shahaab, darling, get up. I know you're not sleeping.'

I sat up but held my head low, not looking at her. Mother put two fingers under my chin and slowly lifted my face. She looked into my eyes and said, 'Shahaab, do you understand what has happened? I think someone has kidnapped Fereshteh. We have to find her. Will you help us?'

Asi said, 'We? Help them? We? But we're dumb and can't talk!'

Mother continued, 'Darling, I'll ask you some questions and I want you to just listen to me. If you want, you can nod your head if I'm right, okay? Did you and Fereshteh only go to the park?' She interpreted the slight movement of my head as a 'no'. 'Did you go somewhere else other than the park?' I pressed my lips together and turned my face away. 'Oh, sorry, I didn't ask correctly. The other place you went to, do you know where it is?' I automatically blinked. Mother seemed very excited. 'Can you take me there?' I think the fear I felt was reflected in my eyes because she asked, 'Are you afraid?' I nodded my head. 'Don't be afraid, I'll be right next to you. I won't let anyone harm you. We can even call your father.' I became more afraid. I pushed her away and freed my face from her hands. 'Okay, okay, we won't tell anyone. It'll be just you and me. I promise. Okay? Will you take me there? You want us to find her don't you? It'll be wonderful if we find her and save her. Everyone will be happy and they'll realize what a good boy you are.'

I didn't care if anyone else other than Mother realized how good I was. She hurriedly changed my dirty, wrinkled shirt and we went downstairs. Fataneh was holding a glass of milk, staring at the stairs. Shadi was trying to drink the milk, but Fataneh wasn't paying any attention and didn't tilt the glass. Mother put on her coat and said, 'Fataneh, stay with Shadi. Shahaab and I will be back soon.'

'Does he know where she is?'

'We'll see.'

'I'll come with you. I'll go crazy if I stay here.'

'No, you can't. What would we do about Shadi? Fereshteh may call too. Someone should be here to answer the phone. I'll be back soon.'

'Can we really trust this child?'

'We can doubt him if you want and I can stay here instead. Who knows if she's even in the same place she went to six months ago with Shahaab.'

'No, no! Please, forgive me. Go ahead, you may find a clue!'

CHAPTER 19

I put my trust in Shahaab. He took my hand and proudly led me down the street. He was happy to be taken seriously, and this overcame his fear. After we passed a few streets his hand began to tremble in mine and his steps became slower.

'What is it, son? Are we there? What's wrong? Are you afraid? Don't worry, I'm right here, just show me the house.'

With a trembling hand he pointed to a building.

'Which one? The red building?' He nodded his head, took a step forwards and pointed to the sign above the building. The market? He nodded again. 'Shahaab, darling, did you come here with someone else? Was it just you and Fereshteh?' He shook his head 'no'! 'Okay, so there was someone else too. Who was it? Was it a man? Will you recognize him if you see him? This is very important.' He nodded 'yes'. 'Good boy. Whoever thinks you're dumb is an idiot!'

I walked to the market. He pulled his hand out of mine.

'What's wrong? Let's go and see what's going on. You can stay right here if you're scared and I'll be right back.'

After I took a few steps he ran up to me and took my hand again. I stopped in front of the market. It was closed. I looked around surprised. I said to myself, What kind of a market is closed at this time of day? 'So what are we going to do now? It's closed. Are you sure this is the right place?' He nodded his head vigorously. 'Very well. There's no one inside. We'll have to wait.' He shook his head. 'Maybe we should come back again later.'

Shahaab seemed nervous. He kept shaking his head and I couldn't understand what he was trying to tell me. I hesitated a bit, then took his hand and started to walk back home. He pulled his hand out of mine and ran back to the market. He pounded on the door with his small fists. I turned back not sure what to do. I said, 'What are you doing? Can't you see it's closed? There's no one here, why are you pounding on the door?' He kept on pounding and kicking the door without paying any attention to me. 'Do you think there's someone here?' He nodded his head, happy that I had finally understood what he was trying to tell me. I began to help by knocking on the glass and the door's metal grille with my keys. I tried to look inside through white curtains that had been carefully pulled together.

A man passed by and said, 'Can't you see it's closed? Go and shop somewhere else!'

I turned away from him and continued to knock on the door. After a while, a woman who lived next door stuck her head out of the window and began complaining, 'What a nerve! Madam, can't you see it's closed? Stop making so much noise!'

'It's an urgent matter.'

'He usually sleeps till past noon.'

'Does he sleep here in the market?'

'Yes, I think so.'

'I'm sorry, but I have to wake him up.'

'Did you leave something here?'

I was glad to have an excuse, 'Yes, everything I own is in my handbag, and I left it here last night.' Shahaab gave me a pleased smile. The woman shook her head, went back inside and shut the window. I continued to knock on the door using my keys. It was no use. I was very disappointed.

Shahaab picked up a white stone from the small pavement garden and used it to hit the grille. I said, 'It's no use. Let's go. We'll come back in an hour.'

He threw another stone angrily. It flew through the grille and shattered the glass. I was stunned and turned around. Shahaab tried to hide behind me. A few moments later a dazed, dishevelled man came to the door. The bright light blinded him. In a hoarse voice he yelled, 'What's going on here? What are you doing?' A couple of passers-by stopped, eager for an argument. I pulled myself together.

The man was searching his keychain for the grille key. He finally opened the door and began yelling again, '*Look what you've done, you bitch!* You have to pay for it. Did you think I'd let you get away with it?' He sprang forwards and grabbed my wrist.

I pulled my hand out of his grip and in a shaking voice said, 'Shame on you!'

'You have to pay for the glass! Who do you think you are?'

'Fine, I will. But first you have to answer my questions. Did a girl named Fereshteh come here yesterday afternoon?'

The man froze. He paused and then said, 'A hundred people come and go here every day. Do you expect me to know their names?'

'But this one's different. This child says you know her pretty well.'

The man looked down and finally noticed Shahaab, who was peeking out from behind me. He was taken aback. He kept looking around. He looked at the people who had gathered around and said, 'What are you staring at? The show's over!' He continued in a quieter voice, 'This kid shouldn't stick his nose in other people's business, plus it's not like he can talk!'

I felt more confident. We had come to the right place. I said, 'So, it seems you know this child pretty well too! And you're mistaken. He doesn't talk to people like you, but he can speak very well to me and to the police.'

Mentioning the police flustered the man. He moved aside and said, 'Come on in. Let's see what you want.'

I entered hesitantly. I was afraid, even though I pretended to be confident.

'I have nothing to say to you. Just tell me where Fereshteh is.'

'How should I know? It's not like all misbehaving runaways come to me.'

'I know she was here.'

'A lot of people come here. I don't know which one she is. As you can see there's no one here now. Take a look.'

I looked around. There was a pillow and a blanket on a bench against the wall. It looked like the man had spent the night there. I walked to the end of the shop, but there was nowhere to hide. I wasn't sure what to do. Shahaab let go of my hand and ran behind the market's main space. The man followed him and I ran after them. It was really dark back there. I couldn't see clearly. I suddenly saw the man standing halfway up some stairs, holding Shahaab, who was struggling, under one arm.

I yelled, 'Let him go, you idiot!'

The man threw Shahaab at me. I caught him in mid-air and with a trembling voice said, 'Are you going to hand Fereshteh over or do you want me to call the police?'

'How do I know you haven't called them already? Or maybe you'll call them later.'

I was now convinced Fereshteh was right here. It seemed like he wanted to make a deal. With a calmer voice I said, 'I don't want to embarrass the girl. I haven't even told her parents yet. If you hand her to me, I'll take her home and tell them she was staying with a friend. I won't mention you because it'll make it worse for the girl. But if she doesn't come with me right away, I'll call every police station in town. You'll wish you'd never laid eyes on her. You had better let her come with me for your own sake. If she comes now it'll be as if nothing's happened. But if this drags on any longer, you'll have to deal with her father and her uncle.'

The man was silent. He was weighing his options. After a few moments he said, 'Fine! But if you mention me, or this market, I won't leave you in peace.'

'Go and get her before anyone arrives.'

The man went up the stairs, opened the door and said, 'Hurry up. Get your things. Get out of here and don't ever come back! Get lost!'

Fereshteh stepped out with her hair in a mess. She stood in the doorway, pale, thin, confused and terrified. An eighteen- or nineteen-year-old boy followed her out of the room. They seemed so young and fragile.

'Oh, Fereshteh! What are you doing here?'

Her voice quivering, she asked, 'Are you alone?'

'Yes. Don't worry. Let's go. Everyone's looking for you. What have you done?'

'I won't come! I'm afraid!'

'Don't be scared. We'll go to our house. I won't let anyone find out where you've been, apart from your mother. I'll say you were upset with her and went to stay with a girlfriend. But then you felt bad and called to let us know.'

Fereshteh gently let go of the boy's hand and walked down the stairs uncertainly. I helped her with her coat and scarf. Fereshteh wept quietly the entire way back. Shahaab proudly held her hand and led her home.

CHAPTER 20

The chaos that had begun the night before changed with Fereshteh's arrival. Fataneh slapped her hard and then passed out. Mother poured water on her face and she finally came to. Fereshteh cried non-stop. Fataneh burst into tears and hugged me for the first time in my life. She kissed me and said, 'God bless you, sweetheart. Fate made you my guardian angel.'

Mother sent Fereshteh to take a bath, and then described the whole story for Fataneh. She listened, terrified and kept pulling at her hair and her face. She finally said, 'Maryam, I'm begging you, please don't say anything to her father. He'll kill her if he hears any of this.'

'Don't worry. We'll say she was upset with you and went to stay with a girlfriend. It got late and she couldn't come back alone in the evening. She decided to annoy you some more so she spent the night there without telling you. She regretted it this morning, called and told us where she was.' My mother's lies were perfect. I was proud of her.

Asi said, 'Nice one! We have such a brave mother. Why can't she stand up to Father and Grandmother?'

Fataneh said, 'Where do you think they are? I am worried about Hossein. His back was really hurting him.'

'They'll call any minute now. I asked Nasser to call us before noon.'

With her hair wet and looking terribly pale, Fereshteh came downstairs and sat across from Mother and Fataneh. Fataneh said, 'What did you do? Didn't you realize what we would go through? Didn't you think of the disgrace?'

Fereshteh started crying and Mother signalled Fataneh to stop speaking. In a loud voice she said, 'Fereshteh, I don't think you're feeling too well. Do you want to have a nap?'

Fereshteh weepily asked, 'What'll happen now?'

Her mother replied venomously, 'What do you think will happen? You've disgraced us! What'll I tell your father?'

'I'll kill myself!'

Mother said, 'What are you talking about? It's not that big a deal. You got into an argument with your mother and childishly ran off to your friend's house without letting anyone know. This morning you regretted it and called us.'

'I'm scared to go home.'

'She's right. Fataneh, let her stay here a few days. She'll come home when things quieten down a bit and her father is less angry.'

'Yes, I think that's a good idea.'

The phone rang and Mother hurried to answer it. In an enthusiastic voice she said, 'Of course we do! We have great news ... Yes, I swear, she's sitting right here in front of me ... Yes, she's fine. She was at a friend's house. She called this morning ... I couldn't tell you because I didn't know where you were.' Mother's tone changed. 'Hello, Hossein. Good news ... What a thing to say! You should be joyful that she's okay ...'

They hung up at the other end. Mother slowly put down the receiver. Fataneh asked, 'What did he say?'

'He's very angry. I don't blame him, but it won't last. We have to keep Fereshteh away from him for a while. Fereshteh, go upstairs and lie down in Shahaab's bed. Stay away from your father for now.'

Fereshteh looked at me. I got up happily, took her hand and led her upstairs. Fereshteh lay down on my bed. I tried to pull the blanket over her.

94

She said, 'Don't!' She burst into tears again. I wasn't angry with her now. I sat next to her and gently caressed her hair. 'I'm ruined. I'm a very bad girl. My father is right to want to kill me.' I shook my head furiously and kissed her wet cheeks. Fereshteh sat up and hugged me hard. 'Shahaab, you're the only one I have. The only person close to me, the only one who knows everything. I am sure that you understood everything. You know I didn't want to go there, I swear to God I didn't! I resisted with all my strength.'

Fereshteh and I began to tremble as soon as we heard the garage door. My uncle walked into the house yelling, 'Where is that good-for-nothing girl?'

Fataneh pleaded with him, 'Hossein, please calm down. She's taking a nap upstairs. Sit down and drink some water.'

'I won't calm down till I kill her! How dare she run away from my house? God knows what she's been up to! I have no use for a daughter who pretends to be at the park and who stays out all night!'

'Brother, calm down. Think of your back. You have to rest or you may become paralysed.'

'How can I rest? They won't let me! I work hard all day for this thankless bunch and see how they treat me in the end!'

Mother said, 'Hossein, it's not a big deal. Sit down and I'll tell you what happened. Don't take it so hard.'

Khosrow started to speak for the first time. 'What do you mean "not a big deal"? Who knows where she's been and who she's been with?'

Fataneh said angrily, 'Be quiet, Khosrow! She was at her friend's house studying all those times, instead of in the park with Shahaab, because she was so annoyed with you pestering her.'

'How can I be quiet? I'm her brother after all.'

Mother said, 'So what? If you were a good brother you wouldn't upset her so much, making her run off to her friend's house.'

'Me? What's it got to do with me? I didn't do anything?'

'You know very well what you've done, stop dragging it out.

95

Hossein, please sit down and drink this. Nasser, help him sit down.'

Throughout all this, Fereshteh was holding me tight, trembling. I could hardly breathe. As the voices downstairs became quieter, Fereshteh's arms turned limp and I was able to pull myself out of her embrace. Fereshteh lay back down on the bed. I slowly went down the stairs, stood next to Mother and held on to her skirt. Touching something that belonged to her comforted me. She said in a gentle tone, 'Hossein, these kids are at a critical age. We have to be flexible with them. It's unbelievable how the smallest things can upset them so much. Their reactions are thoughtless and childish, but they end up regretting it immediately. Fereshteh is a sensitive girl. She got into an argument with her mother and Khosrow had been pestering her too, so she ran off to a friend's house, as she has obviously got into the habit of doing. But then she regretted it and came back. That's all.'

'That's all? I went through hell last night. I almost had a heart attack looking at corpses in the morgue all day, thinking all sorts of thoughts. I died and came back to life a hundred times. And now you say "That's all"?'

'She's a child. She didn't realize what she was doing. You're absolutely right and she'll never do such a thing again. But now, thankfully, it's all worked out okay. Stay calm and be grateful. Think of your health.'

Fataneh handed him the glass and weepily said, 'You're right to be upset. But Maryam's right too. These kids are at a difficult age. She couldn't help herself. She is so miserable now, she kept crying and apologizing.'

'Where exactly was she anyway?'

'At her friend's house as I said.'

'Which friend? Didn't you call them all last night?'

Khosrow stepped forwards and angrily said, 'Father, they're lying! What friend? I called them all myself. What's her name? Give me her address, and I'll go and ask her myself.'

My heart skipped a beat. What if Uncle agreed with him and decided to go along?

Mother's voice trembled a bit, 'Khosrow, stop being a nuisance! Do you think you know all her friends and classmates? I went to her house. They are nice people. I spoke to her mother.'

Hossein was tired but agitated. 'Why didn't they call us yesterday if they're such nice people?'

Mother said, 'Her mother didn't realize you didn't know where she was. She thought Fereshteh had your permission to stay over.'

Khosrow said, 'I swear it's a lie! Where did this friend come from? Why hasn't anyone seen her before?'

'Actually Shahaab knows her. He's gone over there a few times with Fereshteh. He knew the directions to the house and took me there himself. I wouldn't have found it without his help.'

All eyes turned on me.

Khosrow disgustedly said, 'Him? This idiot? I told you it's all a lie! This idiot doesn't know anything. I dare you to take me over there if you can!' He came towards me, grabbed my wrist and dragged me to the front door. Mother and Fataneh looked on, terrified. They didn't know what to do. 'Come on, let's go, dummy. I won't let you go until you show me their house.'

My entire being was filled with rage. Everything he'd ever done to me passed before my eyes. With all the hatred and strength wound up in my small body, I pulled my hand out of his and yelled, 'Your mother is brown, you pimp!'

These were the worst words I knew. In my head I would sometimes use them to swear at mean people. With the silence that followed I realized this time it hadn't been in my head, that I'd actually said them out loud. Khosrow was startled. I stood still for a few seconds, and then ran up the stairs to escape their stares. I needed a quiet place to process what had just happened. I could hear Mother's joyful screams behind me.

'He talked! Did you hear that?'

Uncle chuckled, 'Yes he did! And what a speech!' And he burst out laughing. His laughter was contagious and the others joined in. They kept their composure at first but were soon doubled over. I looked at them with surprise from up the stairs.

Tears were streaming down Uncle's face. He kept wiping them and said, 'Nasser, if this is the way your son's going to talk, maybe it's better if he stays quiet! Otherwise he'll drag our family name through the mud!'

Father was still surprised and couldn't believe it, 'Where did he learn these words?'

'Where all kids learn them.'

I went to my room but Fereshteh was sleeping there and I couldn't be alone with my friends. I opened the door to the balcony. I stood in a corner for a while. From up there I saw my uncle's family leaving. Father held my uncle's arm. He didn't seem angry any more and Fataneh kept thanking him. Khosrow seemed annoyed.

It turned quiet once they had left. I walked up the stairs to the roof and sat down. I was very tired.

Asi said, 'You swore at them.'

'Yes! And they heard! Did a voice come out of my mouth?'

'Did you see how surprised they were? They were all silent. It was as if you'd slapped Khosrow.'

Babi said, 'Those were bad words, weren't they?'

'Yes. Arash's father asked where we'd learned them from.'

I felt light, as if a weight had been lifted from my shoulders. I'd taken a first step. The winter sunlight was very pleasant. Everything seemed beautiful to me. I walked to the edge of the roof and looked at the neighbour's garden that was big and full of trees. Two of the trees with branches that reached our rooftop had leaves on them and all the rest were bare. I'd never seen these trees from above. Their branches seemed fresher and greener from up here. Something moved among the branches. Oh my, there was a nest! I was captivated by it. I heard a noise but was too absorbed in the beauty of these creatures to realize what was going on around me. To get closer to them I pulled myself up the parapet wall as much as I could. I suddenly felt an intense pain in my back. Someone lifted me up. I was struggling in Father's arms. I couldn't understand what had happened. I was shocked. He hit me a few more times. I'm not sure if it was really painful or if the pain I felt was because his blows were unnecessary and unexpected. I still feel this pain every time I look at the stairs leading to the rooftop.

Father put me down. I looked at his angry face with surprise. I couldn't understand why he was so angry. He wagged his finger in front of my face and said, 'Who said you could come up here? Didn't I tell you that no one is allowed up here?'

Mother was standing on the top step and said, 'Thank God you caught him in time.'

'He was hanging from his waist! That was lucky!' He turned to me again and said, 'If I catch you up here one more time, I'll give you a beating you'll never forget. You need a smack on the mouth too' – he gently smacked my mouth – 'for the bad words you said. After this you should only say nice things. Do you understand?'

Mother said, 'Leave him alone. This is not the time.' She took my hand and we carefully climbed down the stairs. 'Nasser, these stairs are very dangerous. We have to do something about them.'

My thoughts were very confused. The shock and bewilderment I felt were being replaced by hatred and anger. The pain of the beating I'd received was becoming greater because it had been so uncalled for. When we reached downstairs I ran into the bathroom and shut the door behind me.

Asi said, 'What an idiot! We had to go on the roof to be alone because Fereshteh is sleeping in our room!'

Babi said, 'They said the rooftop was dangerous.'

'It's not dangerous at all. They don't know how to go up those stairs so they say it's dangerous! Anyway, why did he smack our mouth?'

'He said it was because we'd said rude words.'

'How stupid! People don't get beaten up for saying rude words. He always says "pedar-sag", or "pedar-sookhteh"* himself. The kids on the street use those words too. And whenever

* _Pedar-sookhteh_ literally means 'burnt father' (cursing someone's father to the fires of hell). As a swear word it is synonymous with 'rascal', but it is also used as a term of endearment for small children.

Shadi says "*pedar-sad** khar"† everyone laughs. The only one who gets upset is the person that's being sworn at. He's the one who gets angry. We didn't say rude words to Father, we said them to Khosrow. So why did Father get upset? Is it because he loves Khosrow so much he wants to defend him? Why doesn't he defend us when Khosrow calls us an idiot? He said we should only say nice things from now on. Well, who wants to talk anyway? Especially to him. Remember not to say a word to him ever again!'

* *Pedar-sad* is a childish mispronunciation of *pedar-sag* ('your father is a dog').
† *Khar* is Farsi for 'donkey' (animal names are common swear words in Farsi).

CHAPTER 21

Shahaab's swearing did the job. Fataneh took advantage of the changed atmosphere, took Hossein's arm and said, 'Hurry up. Let's go home. You should lie down.'

Khosrow said, 'What about Fereshteh? Why isn't she coming?'

Fataneh snapped back at him, 'As I said before, it's none of your business. She wants to stay with Maryam a few days to study.'

'Yeah, right! Study!'

'No, actually, she doesn't want to study! I just want her away from you for a few days so she can have some peace and quiet. God knows I'd run away from you too if I could!'

They left and the house turned quiet once again. Nasser lay down on the sofa and said, 'We were lucky it all turned out okay. Who knows what would have happened if we hadn't found her. You can't imagine the things we saw last night. So, did everything really happen the way you described?'

I looked at him with hesitation. I wasn't sure how much of the truth he could handle. My grandmother used to say, 'The less men know the better!' I calmly answered, 'Yes, of course.'

'Where is she now?'

'She's sleeping in Shahaab's room. I don't think she's feeling too well.'

'Does she have a cold?'

'No, she's pale and depressed. That outgoing happy girl has turned into an introvert who's constantly weeping.'

'But why? What's wrong with her?'

'I'm not sure. I think Khosrow pesters her.'

'That's nothing new.'

'Her mother doesn't understand her either. Let her stay here a few days and I'll figure it out. I should go and see how she is. Do you want to come?'

'No. She's really misbehaved and almost killed my brother with stress. I had better remain a bit cool towards her. Did you see Shahaab?!'

'My son spoke! I was right the other time too. He did really call me "Mum".'

'What does it mean then? Can he really speak?'

'Apparently, whenever he feels like it!'

'Wow! He stays silent for ever and then comes out swearing like hell! I really don't understand it. How much can he say? Why won't he speak? What's his problem? He's a complicated child. We should take him to see a psychologist.'

'He doesn't have a problem now that he's started talking. He'll gradually begin saying everything. But that was really funny! It made my heart melt!'

'You should be careful though. If we start laughing at his swearing we'll never be able to control it. It'll get very embarrassing. We have to take it seriously from the beginning. Don't start hugging and kissing him just because he's said something. He has to understand that we'll only be happy if he says nice things.'

'It's really hard though. I want to give him a million kisses!'

'It was very funny, especially with that look on his face. But we have to control ourselves. Where is he anyway?'

'He ran upstairs. I'll get him so we can talk to him.'

Fereshteh said Shahaab hadn't been in his room. We looked for him everywhere, under the beds, in all the rooms and the bathroom. Nasser began to get worried.

'He can't have left the house. He must be upstairs somewhere. What if he's out on the balcony?'

We ran up the stairs again. The door to the balcony was unlocked. Nasser said, 'What if he's gone on the roof?' We looked at each other terrified. The stairs to the rooftop and its low parapet wall were very dangerous. We slowly climbed the stairs. I stopped breathing as soon as I saw him hanging off the parapet wall.

I placed my hand on my chest and froze on the stairs. Nasser walked up to him slowly and quietly. I'm not sure what had attracted Shahaab's attention. He was hanging from the wall trying to reach it. Nasser grabbed him in mid-air and smacked him so he wouldn't dare come up those stairs again.

CHAPTER 22

Things were so hectic at that time that everyone forgot about my swearing, and whether or not I could talk. The important issue was Fereshteh's constant weeping and the things she said to my mother behind closed doors. Fataneh would come over every morning as soon as Arash and Father had left. She would speak to Mother for hours. She cried incessantly. I tried to listen but couldn't figure out what they were talking about. Mother went out by herself a few times. Finally one day, as soon as Father left, Mother got dressed looking very worried. She left Shadi and me with Fataneh, and went out with Fereshteh, who was shaking like a leaf. It was clear they were going out to do something important. Fataneh didn't pay any attention to us at all. She kept pacing, praying and rubbing her hands together. Her anxiety took over the entire house and made me anxious too. What had happened? Where had Mother and Fereshteh gone? What were they hiding? Why didn't Mother tell Father about her excursions? Asi and Babi were quiet.

By noon Mother and Fereshteh weren't back yet. Fataneh kept on pacing the house. It didn't look like she would be giving us lunch. Shadi found a dried piece of bread left from breakfast and tried chewing on it, but I wasn't hungry.

Those terrifying hours finally came to an end, and Mother

came home, helping Fereshteh who was wrapped in a blanket. Fereshteh looked grey and miserable. She was shaking and could barely walk. Fataneh began to cry as soon as she saw them. In an unusually authoritative tone, Mother said, 'Fataneh stop it! I've died and come back to life a hundred times today. See what you made me do!'

They took Fereshteh upstairs and put her in my bed, which had become hers for a while now. Fataneh brought some soup and fed Fereshteh a few spoonfuls. I went to Mother's room. She was lying on her bed. She looked exhausted. After a few minutes she got up and changed her clothes. She gave me a sad smile, caressed my hair and tiredly said, 'Did you children behave yourselves?' I went up to her and hugged her knees. Mother sat down on the bed, hugged me back, and in a weepy voice said, 'I'm not sure how much you know, but I'm sure you were worried too, my dear confidant. You can't imagine what a hard day I've had.' She kissed me, put me down and went to look at Fereshteh through the door. We went down the stairs together.

Fataneh was wiping the kitchen table. 'I'll be in your debt for ever. I don't know what I'd do without you. Why did it take so long? Didn't they say it would only be an hour?'

'You can't imagine what we went through. The baby had grown. They didn't have all the necessary equipment and didn't have an anaesthesiologist either. She bled a lot. We were lucky. We almost lost her. I cursed myself for agreeing to go through with it. If something had happened to her, I couldn't have forgiven myself. If Nasser ever finds out—'

'Thank God it's all over. I know you went through a lot, but if you hadn't been here I wouldn't have been able to do anything. I would have passed out and you would have had to take care of me too! How is she now?'

'The bleeding's stopped but she's very weak. We have to help her get her strength back.'

I understood that they'd been through a dangerous situation and that Fereshteh was scarred in a way, but I couldn't make out how she felt, or how a baby had grown bigger.

Fereshteh stayed with us for another ten days until she felt better. In those days my parents spent most afternoons at Uncle's house and I would stay at home with Fereshteh. She gradually started to talk again. Fataneh brought her schoolbooks over but she wouldn't study. She would open a book and stare into space. Finally, on a Thursday afternoon, she packed her bags and we all went to Uncle's house. Uncle was happy that the rift between Fereshteh, her brother and her mother had been resolved. He kissed her, and Fereshteh cried and apologized. Fataneh was so pleased she kept walking around offering sweets to everyone.

Grandmother, Aunt Shahin and her new husband, as well as Fataneh's mother and her elder sister, Farideh, all came over. Everyone stopped talking of Fereshteh's situation. That was an intimate secret between our family and my aunt.

Grandmother kept complaining that she hadn't seen any of us for a whole month. Everyone kept coming up with an excuse, but no one really answered her. Mother and Fataneh were in the kitchen pouring tea, whispering to one another. Grandmother eyed them suspiciously. Fataneh passed by and gave me a kiss. My uncle laughed each time he looked at me and called me over twice to give me some sweets. Fereshteh offered me pastries and bent down and kissed me on the cheek. She then offered some pastries to Aunt Shahin who said, 'What's going on here? Why is everyone paying him so much attention? Stop spoiling him, he's going to misbehave again . . . '

'Oh no, Auntie, you don't know what an angel he is.'

Aunt Shahin took a pastry, and as soon as Fereshteh moved away she whispered to Grandmother, 'What's going on here? Everyone seems so friendly.'

Grandmother bent her head and with down-turned lips said, 'Thank God. I'm happy as long as these two brothers get along. Let them be happy, it's no skin off my nose.'

Arash was sitting next to Father, looking on as he played backgammon with Uncle. Khosrow called him a few times but Arash shook his head each time and didn't go to his room with him. Khosrow said, 'To hell with you! Let's go, kids.' Babak and Bahram, Farideh's sons, followed him to his room. Bahram turned around halfway up and called me, 'Come along. Khosrow wants to show us something interesting.' I was hesitant because I didn't trust Khosrow at all, but I was also very bored. Aunt Shahin was playing a song and Shadi was dancing, and everyone else was clapping and laughing. Mother was helping Fataneh in the kitchen. Father consulted with Arash before moving his pieces. I looked at them with envy. I wanted him to call me and ask me to sit next to him too. Even if the entire world noticed me and paid attention, I would still crave his attention. I hung my head and slowly followed the boys up the stairs.

Khosrow shut his door and locked it. Just like the time before, he took out a cigarette and matches from his drawer. The kids looked on in awe. Bahram said, 'You're still a kid! You can't smoke!'

'I'm not a kid! I'm three years older than you. I've been smoking for a while. He knows.' He pointed at me. 'But kids can't smoke. This one took a puff and threw up all over my room.'

The boys looked at him with admiration. Khosrow put the cigarette between his lips like a pro and lit it. He opened the window and puffed out the smoke through the screen. Bahram and Babak were amazed by his bravery. We heard voices behind the door and someone turned the handle. Fereshteh said, 'Boys, are you here? I've been calling, why didn't you answer? Supper's ready, come downstairs. Why is this door locked? Hurry up and open it!' Khosrow panicked, threw the cigarette into his wardrobe and said, 'We're coming!' He unlocked the door and said, 'Hurry up, let's go and have supper.'

I'd had too many sweets and wasn't hungry. I took my plate and followed Mother into the kitchen. Everyone had gathered around Fataneh. Fataneh was describing the episode of my swearing without making any connections to the real reason. Mother smiled. Grandmother and Aunt Shahin looked surprised. I panicked. What if they smacked me again like Arash's father had because I'd said a bad word? What if they asked me to repeat what I'd said? Grown-ups were unpredictable. On the one hand they hit you because of what you said, and on the other hand, they laughed and happily recounted it for others! I ran upstairs. A heavy smoke was coming out from under Khosrow's door.

Babi said, 'Ugh! He's smoking again.'

I opened Fereshteh's door. There was no one there. I went inside. As she was packing her things in my room that day, she had said, 'Thanks for sharing your room. You're welcome in my room any time.' I lay down on her bed. Asi and Babi sat next to me.

Asi said, 'You have to learn how to smoke so Khosrow can't show off any more.'

Babi said, 'Yuck! It stinks and makes you sick.'

The sound of yelling and screaming made me jump. Everyone was running around screaming. I walked out of the room. There was smoke everywhere. I couldn't see the stairs. I began to cough. Someone said, 'It's Shahaab! He's up there!' Someone ran up the stairs, picked me up and took me down.

Uncle yelled, 'Everyone go outside! It's dangerous in here!' We all ran out of the house.

Fataneh kept pulling her hair and crying, 'My home! My home!'

Father, Aunt Shahin's husband, Farideh's husband and the boys kept coming and going with buckets of water. After a few moments we heard the fire engine's siren. It was all so entertaining. The red trucks arrived with their long hoses just like in the movies. I had never seen anything so glorious from up close. They put out the fire but kept on pouring white, foaming water everywhere. Furniture was floating on water. Some of the firemen threw the rugs and bedding from Khosrow's room out into the garden. Smoke was still coming out of them. I was having fun and looked on with excitement at all these strange happenings. I carefully walked to the red fire engine. It was filled with strange, interesting things. I touched them. Uncle was sitting on the ground holding his head in his hands. Father was standing next to him. One of the firemen who seemed to be in charge was talking to Father about the fire. Everyone was standing around listening to them.

'I think the fire started in the wardrobe upstairs. Were the kids playing with fire?'

Fataneh came closer and said, 'All the kids were downstairs with us.'

Suddenly everyone turned silent. Grandmother mentioned what seemed to be on everyone's mind. 'Except for Shahaab. He was upstairs.'

They all turned and looked at me. Father looked astonished and Mother turned pale. She stuttered, 'But he doesn't even know how to strike a match! Where did he get matches from?'

Khosrow was hiding in a corner but suddenly stepped forwards and said, 'I have matches in my room! I showed them to him before supper. Didn't I?'

Bahram and Babak looked on in silence.

'I showed him the matches and put them back in my drawer. Babak, I did, didn't I?'

'Yes, he put them in his drawer.'

'Wasn't he standing there looking at me?'

'Yes, but—'

'When we came downstairs for supper, he went back upstairs. He took the matches and started the fire!'

Everyone was silent. I was so confused I couldn't follow what was being said. I was afraid of everyone's mean glances and looked up to Mother hoping to be consoled. But she was even more terrified than I was. Father looked extremely pale.

Grandmother came to herself before everyone else and spoke with a deep vengeance, 'You see, Nasser? Last time you said it wasn't him. That a brick had appeared out of nowhere and hit me on the head. What do you have to say this time? There are all these witnesses now. Take your head out of the sand. This child is dangerous. You have to think of something before he does any more damage or kills someone.' Mother began to cry and ran out of Uncle's house.

Father walked towards me. I felt paralysed and couldn't move. He sat in front of me. He took my arms and squeezed with all his might, shook me and yelled, 'Did you do this? Did you do this, you bad boy?' I kept moving back and forth in his grip. I felt smaller and more helpless than ever before. 'Go on and speak, you bastard. I know you can talk. Tell me what you did!' He gave me a hard slap that made me dizzy. I tasted blood on my lips. I was dying of fear when Fereshteh threw herself at me, hugged me and said, 'Please, Uncle! Stop it! What good will it do? He's still a child.' She handed me to Arash and he took me home without a word.

CHAPTER 23

No one spoke to me in those dark days. I wasn't angry but felt intensely hopeless and alone. I still couldn't believe that anyone could lie so easily. My mother lied sometimes, but her lies were meant to protect me, not destroy me. I slowly understood the meaning of lying, and this understanding made me completely tongue-tied. I didn't even talk to Asi or Babi any more. It was as if they were lost and had left my mind for ever.

My parents argued incessantly. Father took some workers to Uncle's house the next day and said he would pay for everything himself. Mother was angry and said, 'This means you're accepting the fire was Shahaab's doing.'

'Of course it was! Who else could it have been? All those witnesses. He almost killed my poor mother too!'

'He never does anything bad unless someone hurts or upsets him.'

'Stop talking rubbish! Everyone was exceptionally nice to him last night. Fereshteh kept kissing him and my brother kept giving him sweets. Even Fataneh sang his praises. He definitely paid them back! I wish I were dead and didn't have to go through this humiliation! This child is retarded. His actions aren't based on reason and understanding. Even if we assume he does these things to take revenge on those who hurt him it still means he's dangerous. You want to know what I'm really afraid of? What if Shadi annoys him some day? Do you just want to sit there and do nothing, and maybe come home one day to find Shadi dead? Is that it?'

These words terrified my mother and made me shake with fear too. I'd stupidly assumed that Mother's weakness, Father's lack of attention and their occasional arguments, which had begun once they found out I was stupid, had come to an end. But now they all reappeared and intensified. There was no sign of the woman who had single-handedly saved Fereshteh. She didn't protect me any more in the way I expected. It was as if she too had accepted my guilt in the fire incident, and could imagine I was capable of hurting Shadi. With her weakness I became more and more miserable and didn't doubt my own insanity. Imagining that I would one day kill my sister terrified me. I kept obsessing about this thought and it made my hands itch. I would press them together and hide them in my pockets in order to escape from it.

Father came home early one day. Mother dressed me in silence. She took Shadi's hand and we all got in the car. Shadi kept singing songs. Her singing and childish gibberish always drove me mad.

Babi said, 'She's singing to annoy you!'

I was careful to keep my hands from lifting on their own and smashing her head in, but the temptation was getting greater. Once her voice grew loud enough so that I could no longer hear my parents speaking, I couldn't resist any longer. I hit her on the head. She screamed. Mother turned around, scolded me, picked Shadi up and held her on her lap in the front seat. Father gave her a meaningful glance.

Asi said, 'What can we do? We can't help it because we're insane.'

Father asked, 'Why are you so quiet? It's not like we're doing a bad thing taking him to see a doctor. This is our responsibility. We have to be realistic. He has to start school next year and we should know what kind of school to take him to. If we know what the problem is we'll be able to help him better. Maybe if they can find out the extent of his mental deficiency they'll be able to do something about it. I've heard there are international boarding schools for these kinds of kids.'

'What kinds of kids? I still don't believe he was responsible for the fire! Just because he can't speak he gets blamed for everything.'

'When are you going to accept the facts? This child has a problem. Will you believe it if the doctor tells you so?'

'I don't see why no one is willing to understand him. Sometimes I feel like you don't love him at all. Have you ever tried to hug him?'

'As if I have the time! I had to jump through all sorts of hoops just to clear an hour so I could come to the doctor with you. Why do you always confuse the issues? You always want to blame me for everything. He was retarded from birth, do you understand?'

'I believe it's our fault he is the way he is. Maybe we don't pay him enough attention.'

'Why are you giving yourself a guilt trip here? We've treated all our children the same, so why are those other two fine? They're both above average. I work day and night to support my kids, what else am I supposed to do?'

'Maybe your working all the time is part of the problem. We need you. You weren't like this before. You enjoyed spending time with your family, but now you run away from us. I think you're happier away from us. You never want to see this child, it's as if you're embarrassed by his presence.'

'What are you talking about? Stop talking nonsense. I'm just trying to be logical instead of emotional. I'm constantly thinking about what I can do about this sick child. Treating a mental illness takes much longer and is more critical than physical illness. So we need more money and more resources for this child. One of my colleagues said psychiatrists are expensive. I'd like to be able to come home early in the evenings too, but I need to make money. I have to save for his treatment, especially if we need to take him abroad.'

'Abroad? What kind of untreatable illness do you think he has?'

'Maryam, stop arguing! I just meant that I want to be able to provide him with whatever care he needs so I can have a clear conscience in the future. There are special schools for these types of kids abroad.'

'But what exactly do you think is wrong with him? It's not like he has leprosy or cancer!'

'That's exactly the problem with mental illnesses. Nothing seems to be physically wrong. Do you think those who commit murder without any sense of guilt are normal? No! Their illness is a thousand times worse than leprosy or cancer. Maybe if they had been treated in time they wouldn't have become murderers.'

'Can you even hear yourself? Are you comparing our child to a murderer now?'

'Be realistic. He's attempted to kill someone twice already. As parents we are responsible. We can't sit and do nothing until something terrible happens.'

'Stop it! I don't want to hear any more!' Mother began to cry.

'There we go again! I can't talk to you. You can't bear to face reality. No one can criticize this child in front of you. The doctor will clear everything up.'

'I don't want to see the doctor.'

'Be logical! He has a problem. What are you going to do about school next year? No school will accept him the way he is. Why shouldn't we seek help from a specialist?'

The doctor's office was crowded. Mother and Father sat next to each other, and I sat across from them. My heart was racing. The children there all looked strange. One of them was big but was still sitting in a pushchair. His arms and legs were twisted together. Another one was fat and pale, staring at me with half-open, lifeless eyes. His mother kept wiping spit off his face. Fear was added to the other negative feelings I felt inside.

Asi said, 'This doctor will definitely find out we're stupid and retarded. Then he'll take the money Arash's father has saved and send us far away to a special school. They'll lock us up with all these other kids and we'll never see Mother again.'

The thought of being separated from Mother squeezed my heart, even though she too believed I was responsible for the fire. Yes, she must have believed it, otherwise she would have made up a lie and saved me like last time. Like Father, she had really hurt me too.

Babi said, 'They all want to get rid of us. They would prefer it if we weren't around.'

I was sure that one day they would go through with it. Arash's father wouldn't be embarrassed by having a son like me any longer. Then they would all be happy once more. They would talk to each other and never get into an argument again.

Asi said, 'Arash's father has made this plan to get rid of us.'

Babi said, 'If the doctor agrees with Arash's father then there's nothing we can do. They'll send us away to school.'

Mother got up, took Shadi's hand and went towards the toilet. She gently asked, 'Shahaab, do you need to go too?'

I shrugged my shoulders. She asked this question a hundred times a day. She and Shadi continued to the loo. Father was reading a newspaper. I quietly got up and walked out of the doctor's office.

CHAPTER 24

The street was crowded and all the people looked big and tall to me. To see their faces I had to tilt my head back all the way. They surrounded me like a wall. I walked aimlessly in the direction most people were going. The weather was cold and cloudy. Drivers were undecided about whether it was too soon to turn on their headlights. I walked by bright shop windows but their displays didn't interest me. My heart was filled with sadness and my throat felt restricted. I'd always been afraid of being abandoned, but now I had left on my own. I kept talking to Asi and Babi.

Babi was frightened and said, 'Where are you going to go now? You'll get lost! Turn back, let's go home.'

Asi said, 'No, they won't take us home. They're going to send us somewhere far away. Don't be scared, I'm right here.' But his voice shook with fear too.

Sometimes people would look at me and say something, but I would hurry past them so they wouldn't realize I didn't know how to talk. I crossed a busy intersection and turned on to a darker street with fewer shops. The crowd was thinner here. It was almost dark now. I was very afraid and my feet ached. I kept swallowing the lump in my throat but tears flowed down my face uncontrollably. I felt so alone. I wished someone would recognize me and take me home. I was cold and hungry. I leaned against a wall feeling abandoned and unwanted. No one loved me. Even Mother, my final source of hope, had surrendered and wanted to send me away. I was so deep in thought that I didn't realize where the lady came from. With a gloved hand she caressed my hair and kindly said, 'Why are you crying, child?' She knelt in front of me. 'What's your name? What's wrong? Are you lost? Where's your mother?'

I began sobbing and pointed in the direction I had come from. The kind lady took my hand and began walking in that direction.

'Look carefully. Pay attention and let me know if you see your mother.'

We hadn't reached the end of the street yet when she stopped. She knelt beside me again and said, 'Listen, dear, you need to tell me your name. Do you know your address?'

I looked at her in silence.

Babi said, 'She hasn't realized we're stupid and can't talk.'

The lady got tired of waiting and said, 'I don't know what to do. You won't talk and I'm in a hurry. Wait here until your parents come and find you.' She let go of my hand and left. I felt as if I was drowning and the last lifeboat was floating away. Fear overcame me. I ran after her, took a corner of her skirt and looked at her with pleading eyes. She slowed down. She knelt again and said, 'If you want me to help find your mother, you need to tell me your name and address. What's your name?'

I looked at her with weepy eyes. She took a deep breath and stopped pressuring me. She took my hand and walked to where a group of people had gathered around a policeman. In that chaos I couldn't hear what she said to the policeman. He stepped forwards and asked my name, my address and my father's name.

The woman said, 'I think he's deaf.'

'What a situation. You have to take him to the station, ma'am.'

'But I have a lot to do, officer! I've been walking around for an hour because of this boy. I have guests and I'm late. They'll get worried.'

'What am I supposed to do? I'm on duty now and need to

attend to these gentlemen. I can't keep this child here with me in the cold.'

'I can't go to the station either. This child won't let go of me. Do you think they'll take care of him there?'

'Definitely not as well as you can!'

He turned back to the men surrounding him. The woman started thinking. After a few moments she entered the crowd and walked up to the policeman again. She called him several times until he finally noticed her.

'Officer, this child is tired and hungry. He trusts me. I can't just leave him at the station. If you think it's okay I'll take him home, and leave my name and number with you. If his parents show up, tell them to pick him up from my house.'

The policeman nodded and turned back to the crowd. The woman took me to a car parked on another street. She let me in the back seat and got in the driver's seat herself. She took out a pen from her handbag and wrote some things down on a piece of paper and said, 'Stay here. I'll give this address to the policeman and be right back.'

I was afraid she would leave me and go away. I wanted to follow her but the car was comfortably warm and gave me a sense of security. I was so confused and tired that I fell asleep as soon as the car began to move.

CHAPTER 25

Shahaab wasn't there when I got back from the toilet. I looked around distractedly and asked Nasser, 'Did you send Shahaab somewhere?'

'Wasn't he with you?'

'No. He was sitting right here. Didn't you see where he went?'

'No!'

At first we looked around the doctor's office, slightly annoyed. But soon we started to get worried. We ran out on the street and searched the surrounding shops and buildings. We kept asking passers-by about a five-year-old boy wearing a dark blue coat and a red and blue knitted cap. There was no sign of him. We kept running around distressed. Nasser got in the car. He was anxious and upset. He said, 'Get in, let's drive around.'

I was crying as I got in. 'What scared him? What did you do to him?'

'Me? What did I do? He's mad, there's no reason for what he does.'

'That's not true! I knew he was upset but couldn't say anything. He's sad and you never show him any kindness.'

We walked and drove around until it got dark. Nasser kept chewing on his moustache and I couldn't stop crying. Shadi realized something was wrong and sat quietly in the back seat. She seemed worried too.

119

'What if someone has kidnapped him? He was afraid to go anywhere alone. How could he have gone so far away? Where could he be? Oh my God! It's getting dark and my poor child is tired and hungry! What's become of him?'

We didn't have a choice but to go to the police station. We filled out all the necessary forms and they made some calls. The officer in charge was a kind man. He said with compassion, 'Don't worry. We'll find him. Go home. I'll let you know as soon as we hear anything.'

Arash came to the door as soon as he heard us walk in.

'What's wrong, Mum? Why did it take so long?'

I went up the stairs still weeping. Nasser looked stressed and upset. He placed Shadi, who had fallen asleep in the car, down on the couch. With a hoarse voice he said, 'Shahaab's missing.'

'What do you mean, "missing"? Wasn't he with you?'

'We were sitting in the doctor's office. Your mother went to the lavatory and I was reading the paper. I thought he'd gone to the loo with your mother. But apparently he walked out and we don't know where he is now.'

'Let's look for him!'

'What do you think we've been doing all this time? We've informed the police too. They said they would call us if they heard anything.'

I came down the stairs agitated. 'I can't just sit here. I'll go out and search for him.' I was shaking all over.

Arash stepped forwards. 'I'll come too. Poor Shahaab can't speak. How will they know he's ours if they find him?'

'Maryam, calm down a bit. Where are you going to go? We looked everywhere. Eat something. I'll go to the station to see if they've heard anything.'

We all froze when the phone rang. Nasser picked it up quickly.

Fearful and hopeful at the same time, I pressed my hand against my mouth to keep from screaming, 'Is it from the station?'

'No ... Hi, brother ... No, we just got home ... Shahaab's missing, we were looking for him.'

Five minutes later Hossein and his family were at our door.

'What happened?'

'I don't know what to do!' And for the first time Nasser's eyes filled with tears. He put his head on Hossein's shoulder and wept.

Fataneh sat next to me and held me. 'They'll find him. I promise.'

Fereshteh was standing by the door looking on with worried, weepy eyes. Khosrow asked Arash, 'Is he really missing?'

Hossein said, 'Explain everything. Where did you lose him? What time was it?'

Nasser briefly went over everything. I kept praying while terrible thoughts went through my head. 'My poor innocent child! We hurt him so much he ran away. He would never go anywhere without me, and now he's run away. He chose to leave us! Can you imagine how upset he must have been to choose to leave by himself? We were so unkind to him! Fataneh, believe me when I tell you it's been at least a year since his father hugged or kissed him.'

Nasser said bitterly, 'It's not my fault. He didn't like it when I tried to hold him. It was as if I were a stranger. He was actually kinder to strangers. Sometimes he stared at me as if he hated me. And sometimes he would pretend I wasn't even there.'

'Because you never paid any attention to him or showed any kindness! Did you think he wouldn't notice? My poor innocent child was like a thorn in your side, and your mother's. Every time she sees us she has to mention something about his being retarded or insane. And you believe her. I swear Shahaab heard and understood everything. We were taking him to the doctor today at Nasser's insistence, and he hates doctors. He stopped playing from the day of the fire. He was so depressed I couldn't bear to look at him. I tried to distract him with different things, to make him happy, but it was useless. I couldn't believe a child could be sad for such a long time. Where is my poor helpless child now in this cold? He'll freeze if he stays out on the street! What if someone's kidnapped him? I've heard they kidnap children and sell their kidneys!'

Fereshteh began to sob out loud. Fataneh said, 'God forbid! Stop saying these things! I can't imagine what you're going through, but you should trust in God.'

'I have to look for him. I can't just sit here.'

'It's eleven o'clock now and we've searched everywhere.'

'What if he's somewhere on the street?'

Hossein said, 'She's right. We'll hunt around. It's better than sitting here.'

'What if they call from the police station?'

'The kids will stay here and we'll check in every half-hour.'

CHAPTER 26

The unfamiliarity of the room scared me when I woke up in the morning. I hid my head under the blanket. Remembering the events of the previous evening filled my heart with sadness, but this was immediately replaced with a great feeling of fear. I came out from under the blanket and looked around the room with curiosity. It was a large, bright room. On one side there were a wardrobe, a dresser, and a bookcase made of white wood. On the other side were a large desk with several drawers, a desktop calendar, a paper holder, and a brown leather cup holding pencils and pens. The purplish-pink curtains and bedcover shone under the light coming in from the window above the bed. I liked the room. It had everything but seemed like it hadn't been used in a long time.

I sat on the bed. I missed Mother. It was the first time in my life that I'd woken up without her near to me. My throat felt tight. I heard a noise from outside. I looked through the window above the bed and saw a large, tree-filled garden. Then I noticed the dolls arranged in front of the mirror; so many beautiful dolls. I got out of bed and picked one of them up. I was absorbed in the doll with its blue glass eyes when the door opened and the lady from the previous night came in. I dropped the doll in fear, jumped into bed and pulled the blanket over my head. She sat next to me laughing, and caressed me from over the blanket.

'Wake up, dear. You were so tired last night you didn't even have any supper. Let's wash your face and have some breakfast.'

I still didn't dare come out from under the covers. She slowly pulled them aside and continued with a smile, 'Get up, sweetheart. Don't be scared.'

I looked at her kind eyes and smiling face. She looked older than she had last night. Her hair was a beautiful colour, almost blonde like the doll that was lying on the floor now. She had a pale lipstick on her lips. Mother rarely wore lipstick. The woman was wearing a long, loose floral dress that reminded me of a garden. No, I wasn't afraid of her. I got out of bed, took her hand and walked to the bathroom.

'Good boy. Can you wash yourself or do you need help?'

I shook my head, walked into the bathroom and shut the door.

Babi said, 'She doesn't realize we're older now and can wash ourselves.'

An older man was at the breakfast table reading the papers. I was surprised to see him. I hadn't expected anyone else to be in the house. I hid behind the woman. She said in a happy voice, 'Good morning! We're here!'

The man laid down the papers and said, 'Oh my, what a cute little boy you've found! How are you, son? What's your name?'

He was kind too. I could recognize kindness at a glance.

Asi said, 'They don't know we're dumb and can't talk, that's why they like us.'

The lady said, 'Don't pester him, I don't think he can talk. We'll call him our "little prince", how's that?' She laughed. 'So what do you think? Do you like it?'

Babi said, 'The "little prince", like in the cartoon.'

I gave a shy smile.

'He likes it. So this little boy likes the "little prince" and it's okay if we call him that. Very well, sit down and have some breakfast now.' The woman constantly talked and made little pieces of bread and butter for me.

The man said, 'Remember what a fuss Nastaran used to make just to eat a mouthful?'

'Yes, but Keyvan on the other hand was such a good eater.'

'No, you've forgotten. When he was the same age as this little prince he would make a fuss too. He became a good eater once he got a bit older.'

'Remember how I'd line up the morsels like a train and make whistling noises just so they'd open their mouths and let the train into the tunnel?'

'Yes, do the same thing with this lovely chap.'

'No, this little prince is a good boy and eats his food.'

After breakfast the woman began collecting the dishes and clearing the table. The man got up, set aside the papers, interlocked his fingers and stretched. He asked, 'Soudabeh, do you need anything from the shop?'

'Get some milk and ice cream.'

'Ice cream in winter?'

'Kids like ice cream.'

'Oh, okay. I'll take him along.'

'Good idea, like in the old times when you used to take Keyvan.'

'Yes, those were good times. Okay, little prince; put on your coat, let's go to the shop. Do you want to come with me?'

I shyly nodded my head and went to get my coat from the bedroom.

When I got back the man was standing by the kitchen speaking to the woman. 'Don't you think it's strange we haven't heard from his parents yet?'

'No, it hasn't been that long.'

'Poor child. He's so sweet. Do you think he can't talk at all or is he just staying silent with us?'

'I think he can't talk. Otherwise he would have said something last night when he was so scared, tired and cold.'

'Maybe he was tongue-tied with fear, because he clearly hears and understands everything.'

'I don't know. Whatever it is, he's obviously upset about something. His eyes are very sad.'

'That's natural. I'd be sad and frightened too if I were lost.'

'No, it's more than that.'

The man turned around and noticed me. He laughed and said, 'Little prince! You're back! You've found your hat and coat, but I haven't shaved yet. We'll shave together when we get back, okay?'

The man took my hand. I felt safe. After a while we got to a park. The man asked, 'Do you want to play in the park?' And without waiting for my response, he led me to the playground. He helped me sit on a swing and pushed me. Then he sat on a bench and looked at me with a sad smile. I felt I had to do something to make him happy, so I ran up the highest slide. I wanted him to see that I was quick and agile. I don't know why it was so important for me to gain his approval. I waved to him, and he smiled and waved back. I bravely came down the slide and he clapped for me. When we left the park he said, 'Let's go shopping for Soudabeh now.'

The shopkeeper said, 'Congratulations, Mr Karimi, you have a kid!'

'Yes I do! And what's wrong with that?'

'At your age, nothing, as long as he's your grandchild! Is he?'

'I wish! If I had a grandchild like this little prince I wouldn't need anything else.'

Asi said, 'Like us?! He wants a child like us? He's so stupid. He doesn't know we're retarded.'

The man bent down, picked me up and held me in front of the counter.

'Little prince, do you want some sweets or a chocolate bar?' I wasn't used to so much kindness so I hung my head. He kissed my cheek. 'Don't be shy. Come on, tell me. My back's aching and I want to put you down, you're heavy!' I worried about his aching back and tried to get down. He put me down, surprised. 'What happened? You don't want me to hold you?' I shook my head. 'Are you worried about my back?' I happily nodded my head several times. The man looked at me with great kindness and caressed my hair. 'What a lovely child! Okay then, Javad,

126

choose something tasty yourself, and give me some milk and ice cream too.'

Javad put the milk and other things in a plastic bag and said, 'Mr Karimi, you didn't say whose child this was.'

Mr Karimi went over everything in a hushed voice. I knew he was talking about me but I was grateful that he did it in a low voice. Arash's father always talked in a loud voice, even when he was saying bad things about me. He thought since I couldn't speak, I couldn't hear either. I don't know why this man, who I now knew was called Mr Karimi, reminded me of Arash's father even though they were so different. Maybe it was because I wished Arash's father would pay attention to me like Mr Karimi did. He talked to me the entire way back and showed me interesting things.

When we got back, Soudabeh greeted us and took the bag into the kitchen. As she was taking off my coat she said, 'I made you spaghetti for lunch.' She turned to Mr Karimi. 'Remember how the kids loved spaghetti more than anything else? You can have some of the rice from last night.'

'I'll have some spaghetti too. Any news?'

'No!'

We ate lunch laughing and happy. Soudabeh gave me the last few spoonfuls whistling and pretending they were carriages on a train, just the way Mother sometimes did when she fed Shadi.

After lunch Soudabeh washed the dishes and Mr Karimi put me on the bed next to him. He spoke to me of his children. I enjoyed the deep sound of his voice. Then Soudabeh took me to the pink bedroom, laid me in bed and said, 'This is Nastaran's room. I can't bring myself to change anything here. She likes to see her room the way it was every time she comes back to Iran. Nastaran always loved books even when she was a little kid. Let me see if I can find one for you.' She pulled out a thin book and handed it to me. It had beautiful pictures that I'd never seen before. Mother's books were all repetitive and she was rarely in the mood to read to me. Soudabeh, however, read me the whole story. When she finished I closed my eyes and pretended to go to sleep, so I wouldn't bother this kind woman any more. She was sleepy herself and had nodded off a few times as she was reading to me. I also wanted to be alone for a bit. After she left the room I opened my eyes.

Babi said, 'Where is Mum now? Do you think she misses us too?' My throat felt constricted. 'What is Arash's father doing now? He's probably happy that we're lost. Are they even looking for us? Shadi is probably sleeping in our bed.' I pressed my head against the pillow and burst into tears.

CHAPTER 27

The following day we went to the police station with Nasser and Hossein. Their shifts had changed. We went over everything once more. The officer in charge sent us home and promised to call as soon as he had any news.

I was lying on the sofa listening to the children talking in Arash's room, 'Mother's right. Something must have happened to him. If a decent person had found him they would have taken him to the station by now and we would have heard something. They must have kidnapped him.'

Fereshteh started to sob, 'He was such a good boy. If it hadn't been for him you lot would never have found me. I owe my life to him.'

Khosrow responded with anger and ridicule, 'Shut up. I would have found you myself. It's not like the retard was Superman!'

Arash yelled, 'He wasn't dumb at all. You're the one who gave him this nickname. He was always sad because you bullied him so much.'

'I had nothing to do with him being sad. Everyone in your house is sad. Your mother's always depressed, she never says anything and rarely laughs. And your father's never at home, and when he is, he's angry or tired. And you're constantly studying in your room. Actually, whenever I come here I get depressed too. In our house

129

we all argue, yell at each other and sometimes get smacked by Father, but at least he talks to us and sometimes tells jokes.'

By noon the entire family had gathered in our garden. I didn't even have the energy to talk any longer. Fataneh took care of the guests and described the events for the newcomers. Fereshteh had locked herself in Shahaab's room. It wasn't clear if Grandmother was more upset about Shahaab or her own son. She kept saying, 'What's my son going through! My Nasser has aged so much!'

Farideh arrived, hugged me and said she was sure the police would find Shahaab.

The doctor came and gave me an injection to calm me down. I was unwilling to go upstairs, afraid that I would miss something. They took me to Arash's room and laid me down on the bed. I carefully listened to all the voices outside.

Shahin said, 'How did you lose him? He never dared go anywhere without his mother.'

Farideh said, 'They must have kidnapped him.'

With her contradictory feelings about Shahaab, Grandmother said, 'God forbid! Who would want a deaf and dumb child anyway?'

Fataneh explained, 'He was very upset after he set fire to our house. They were taking him to see a doctor and he ran away . . .'

Bahram reproached Khosrow, 'You have to tell them it wasn't him. It's not fair, you have to tell them!'

I sat up and listened carefully.

'How do you know it wasn't him? We weren't there. Maybe he went upstairs again, took my matches and started the fire.'

'That's not true. You know that the fireman said the fire started in your wardrobe, then spread to your clothes and the rest of the room.'

I walked out of the room. Nasser, Hossein and Arash were sitting at the dining table but they were listening to the boys too. Nasser got up, walked over to Bahram and said, 'Bahram, tell me what you know? What happened that night?'

Khosrow panicked. 'Nothing happened. He's imagining things. He thinks you'll find Shahaab if he makes up these stories.'

'Even if we don't find him at least we'll know what really happened. He was very upset. The poor child can't speak, but you boys can, so it's your responsibility to tell the truth.'

They were all silent. Then I heard Bahram's determined voice. 'I wanted to say something from the start. I was very upset at first, but then I thought that Shahaab doesn't understand anything and it's all over and done with. So I let it go. I didn't want to make a fuss and upset Aunt Fataneh. But when I heard that Shahaab was missing I knew he'd run away because he was upset for getting blamed for the fire.'

'So tell me what happened that night.'

Everyone was staring at Bahram. Khosrow took advantage of the opportunity and quietly slipped away.

'We were all in Khosrow's room before supper. Khosrow lit a cigarette. Just for fun. He wasn't going to smoke it. Then Fereshteh came to the door and asked why it was locked. She wanted us to open it. Khosrow panicked and threw the cigarette into the wardrobe and we all ran out of the room. I thought the cigarette was out. But half an hour later the wardrobe caught fire.'

Nasser had turned red. 'And I punished my innocent child in front of everyone!' He turned around, sat down at the dining table and held his head in his hands. His shoulders heaved. Everyone was in shock. I felt like my son had been found not guilty after he'd already been executed.

CHAPTER 28

That afternoon Soudabeh made Mr Karimi go up a ladder and bring down all their old suitcases from the attic. She looked through them one by one and finally found what she was looking for.

'Aha! Found it! I knew I hadn't thrown it out. Remember this shirt and jacket? We brought it for Keyvan from London. It looked so good on him.'

'Yes, I remember. How time flies! It was like yesterday, when we put it on him and took him to your sister's.'

Asi said, 'They love their children, so why did the children run away?'

Babi said, 'They probably don't know their parents love them so much.'

Mr Karimi gave me a bath. He filled the tub. I stayed in the warm water for a while and he talked of his kids. It was as if they had nothing else to talk about. We played with the water, made bubbles and laughed. Soudabeh was waiting at the door with a towel. She dried me and looked over my body. She whispered to her husband (she didn't realize that I had really good hearing and could hear her), 'He doesn't have any scars.'

She dressed me in clean, beautiful clothes that smelled slightly of mothballs. She combed my hair. She took a few steps back and looked at me admiringly, 'You are truly a beautiful child. And in these clothes you look like such a gentleman! Karimi, come and take a look!'

'Oh my!'

That night we went out to their friends' house. I was the focus of the party. Everyone looked at me curiously. They smiled kindly and sometimes stroked my head, but I was very embarrassed. I couldn't lift my head. I chewed on my lips so much they were sore. The kids, who were all older, gathered around me. Souda-beh said, 'Kids, this is my lovely little boy. His name is "little prince". Go and play with them, dear. Nazanin, will you take care of him please? Play with him in your room, okay?'

I looked at her. She looked just like Fereshteh. I took her white hand and went to her room.

Over supper one of the ladies said, 'What strange parents! Aren't they looking for their child? Haven't they gone to the police yet? We would have taken over the station by now!'

Soudabeh gestured to the woman to stop talking in front of me. She gave me a kiss. She put some food on a plate for me and took me to a corner of the room. She sat me down on a sofa and fed me, but I'd lost all my appetite. I felt very sad.

That night I fell asleep in the car on the way back. I woke up before everyone else the next morning. The room wasn't strange to me now, but I missed my own room and my mother's voice. I hid my head in the pillow and wept.

At breakfast Soudabeh said to Mr Karimi, 'This child is upset. He wants his mother. He was crying this morning. Let's take him to the police station.'

'What was the name of the officer you talked to?'

'Shokouhi.'

'I'll call Information and get the number for the station. I'll talk to him and see what we should do.'

After several calls, Mr Karimi was finally able to get through to the station. I nervously observed all he said and did. My heart was beating fast.

'Hello, I wanted to speak to Officer Shokouhi, please ... He's not there? How can I reach him? . . . Tomorrow? . . . No that'll be too late. I have an urgent matter. Can I speak to whoever is in charge please? . . . What? Is the station closed at weekends? . . . Okay, I'll call back in an hour.'

Soudabeh was as excited as I was. She asked, 'What did he say?'

'Nothing, just what you heard. It's the weekend. They barely do their jobs on weekdays, let alone the weekend! Shokouhi isn't on duty today.'

'So what do we do now?'

'Nothing, we've done all we could. We've found a child, we've informed the station and given them our phone number and address in case his parents show up. What else can we do? Why are you so worried? They're the ones who should be worried. What parents! We're having fun here, aren't we? Are you tired of the little prince?'

'Not at all! I love having him here. It'll be so sad when they come to take him away.'

'Get ready now, we have to go and pick up Mahmoud.'

'What if they call and we're not here? Let's go to the police station and check things out.'

'The police station? No way! Remember the time we took that man who'd had an accident? Remember how they treated us? They took me to jail before they realized I was just trying to help and hadn't been involved in it! Thank God the chap lived and was able to tell them I was innocent, otherwise I would have been executed over nothing! I swore right there and then that I'd never go to a police station willingly again.'

'You're exaggerating. It wasn't as bad as all that.'

'It wasn't? You've forgotten . . . '

'Anyway, what are we going to do about this child?'

'Nothing. We'll wait until there's some news.'

'But it's been two days already. What if they've called when we weren't in?'

'They would have left a message if they had. I've been check-ing the answering machine. We're not the ones who should be searching for them; they should be searching for their child. Hurry up and get ready now.'

'Where are we going anyway?'

'We made a plan to go walking at Darakeh with Mahmoud last night. We'll have lunch there. You can call Mahnaz to join us too. Their kids got along with the little prince last night.'

We went for a walk on that bright winter day. We played and laughed. I ate more than ever. I didn't even think about Asi and Babi. It was as if I didn't need them. But at night, when Soudabeh turned off the lights, all the sadness in the world pressed down on my chest and I wept soundlessly. Why weren't they looking for me?

The next morning I felt as if I couldn't breathe without my mother any longer. I even missed Shadi and Arash. I started to cry. Soudabeh came into the room. She picked me up and took me to their room. Mr Karimi was awake, stretching on the bed. Soudabeh admonished him. 'Get up. Can't you see how upset he is? We have to find his parents. Today is Monday and everyone is back at work.'

'Let's wait till after we've eaten at least. What's wrong, child? Don't be sad. I'll go to the station for your sake. But the whole world has turned upside down! Instead of them looking for us, we're looking for them!'

After breakfast Mr Karimi got dressed, kissed my cheek and said, 'Don't you worry, I'll find them wherever they are.' He turned to Soudabeh. 'It's your fault if anything happens to me.'

'Like what? Don't worry, nothing's going to happen to you. I'm sure everyone will be grateful to you.'

'I really don't like going to the station. I don't know how to talk to those people. I'm their fathers' age, but they expect me to be respectful and call them "sir"! In the end they'll blame us for everything, just wait and see!'

'Don't make such a fuss. They're very nice and polite. Get going now.'

CHAPTER 29

Two days went by. With every shift change we would go to the station and describe the situation to the new shift. The officers would review the files, we would leave our phone number and address, and then go back home again. I was feeling worse hour by hour. Even the police were more worried now.

At the weekend the officer in charge told Hossein, 'The situation has changed. It's no longer a simple case of a missing child. The possibility of it being an abduction is greater now. When someone finds a child, they usually take him to the police station immediately, unless they have a sinister intention. Sometimes if there's a problem and they can't do it immediately, they return him within a couple of days. I hope this child hasn't been abducted by criminals. Children who don't speak and have mental defects are more in danger. Sociopaths and even people with slight problems are tempted to kidnap these types of children because they're sure there's no threat of being found out. They can do whatever they want to the child.'

They didn't tell me all that was said that day, but Nasser heard everything and was very disturbed. It was a living nightmare. I couldn't cry any more. I kept staring at a corner, imagining terrible things. Arash fed Shadi, who hadn't been washed in days. The house was in total disorder. Fataneh came over and cleaned up a bit, and brought us some food, which we didn't touch. Nasser couldn't bring himself to do anything. He didn't even shave. He went through our photo albums all night, searching for a large, distinct photo of Shahaab.

'How strange, we have so few pictures of him. All the pictures are of you and Shadi.'

Early Monday morning he headed to several newspaper offices and gave them Shahaab's information as a missing child.

CHAPTER 30

When Mr Karimi informed the police why he was there at the station, everyone gathered around and started asking him questions. He was finally directed to the chief officer. The officer excitedly asked, 'You've found Shahaab Mokhtari? Did I hear you right? Please tell me everything one more time.'

'Actually I don't know what his name is because he can't speak. But he fits your description.'

'Where have you been all this time, sir? Didn't you think how worried his family was? What thoughtless people! You have to answer for your actions, sir!'

Mr Karimi turned pale and shaking with anger said, 'I knew it! I knew I shouldn't have come here. I'm even being blamed! We found the child in the dark and cold, took him to a police officer, and following his advice, took the child who wouldn't let go of my wife, home. We gave all our information to the police. We have pampered him for three days the way I'm sure they've never done at his own home. We waited for news from the station. We called, and no one gave us a clear answer, and now that I'm here looking for his thoughtless parents, instead of being thanked I'm being blamed!'

'When did you go to the police?'

'The night my wife found him. She went to a police officer.

138

He took her name and number, and said he'd call us whenever he heard from the child's parents.'

'Which officer was this?'

'Officer Shokouhi, on Karim Khan Street. On Friday at nine in the evening.'

'Oh . . . Officer Shokouhi? He's been on sick leave for a few days.'

'How long has he been sick? Since Friday, I bet, because my wife is sure that was his name.'

'You wait here. Let me check.'

The chief officer came back after a few minutes and apologized to Mr Karimi, saying, 'You can't imagine what his parents have gone through. I was worried his poor mother wouldn't make it. Please bring the child to me and I'll call them to come here.'

Everyone seemed to have an excuse for everything. Apparently Officer Shokouhi had been buried in work on that rainy night. He had had to make sense of a chaotic situation despite a terrible sore throat and headache. When he had finally got back to the station he couldn't even stand up any more. He had put all his paperwork in a drawer and angrily told the shift officer, 'I'm sick and tired of this job! We have to deal with people in the worst situations. They call us during tragedies, arguments, betrayals, murder and other crime. No one calls us when they're happy enjoying life!'

When he got home he had gone straight to bed with a high fever and dreamed of crime the entire night. The next morning his wife had called the station to say he was sick and wasn't coming to work for a few days.

CHAPTER 31

Mother, Arash holding Shadi's hand, Fereshteh, Fataneh, Khosrow and even my uncle were waiting impatiently in front of the police station. But I couldn't see Father anywhere. Mr Karimi hadn't stopped the car yet when Mother opened the door and pulled me into her arms. I laid my head against her shoulder and cried. Her smell was comforting to me. I noticed the others after a few moments. I was happy to see them all and let them each give me a kiss, including Khosrow.

Fereshteh pleaded, 'Please don't do such a thing ever again! Your parents almost died from grief.'

Asi said, 'Even Father? He didn't even look for us.'

After the first few emotional moments everyone noticed Mr and Mrs Karimi. They were looking at us with teary eyes. Mother stepped forwards and took Soudabeh's hand, 'Thank God you found him. You can't imagine what we went through. I had never spent a night apart from him before. I went through hell and back!'

Mr Karimi looked around and asked, 'Where is his father?'

'He's in the station having a fit. He can't help himself – he almost went mad these past few days.'

Babi said, 'Is he fighting with them because they found us?'

Soudabeh said to Mother, 'You should pay alms to show your gratitude for his return.'

Mother held me tight. 'I will. I prayed non-stop and made many promises to God.'

Father stepped out of the station, livid. His face opened up a bit when he saw me. He turned to Mother and said, 'Here's your son, madam.' He tried to hug me but I held on to Mother. Father's outstretched arms dropped, and he just kissed the back of my neck. He thanked Mr and Mrs Karimi. Mrs Karimi said, 'I truly congratulate you. Shahaab was a very good boy, just like a true little prince. We've really become attached to him. Would you allow us to visit him sometimes? We'll miss him.'

'Of course. It's very kind of you.'

Mr Karimi stretched out his arms and I leaped into them. He whispered in my ear, 'See, I didn't break my promise and found them for you. Are you happy now?' I circled my arms around his neck. 'Do you want me to come and take you to the park sometimes?' I nodded. He kissed my cheek and put me down. 'Goodbye for now, little prince.'

After saying goodbye we each went towards our cars. I held Mother's hand and kept turning around to wave at Mr and Mrs Karimi. They looked sad. Soudabeh still had tears on her face.

Babi said, 'They have to go back home now. They loved us and will miss us, just like they miss their children.'

I felt sad. I pulled my hand out of Mother's and ran towards them. I kissed Mr Karimi's face and ran back to Mother again. Father was surprised by this unusual behaviour and looked at me strangely. It was as if I'd given him a hard slap.

CHAPTER 32

Soon everything went back to normal. Arash was busy with school and his multiple extra classes. Father came home even later to make up for the time he'd lost at work. Shadi was happy and cute, constantly babbling sweetly. And Mother was busy with housework, which had increased with the approaching New Year. But something had changed. Everyone treated me nicely and behaved more carefully around me, but there was a question in everyone's eyes, wondering what had happened to me in those days away from home. Wondering if I would run away again. I tried to ignore it but I felt something had changed inside me. Those few days away from home had exposed me to a new world. I kept comparing our house to Mr and Mrs Karimi's. Theirs seemed brighter and cosier. They joked with one another and looked at each other with kindness in their eyes. They seemed happier and more alive than us even though everything reminded them of their kids and brought tears to their eyes. Soudabeh sang as she did her chores and you could tell from her face that she enjoyed what she was doing. Mother, however, always frowned while she worked. It was clear she hated what she was doing and was only doing it out of necessity. In those days I came to believe that if Mother could have been a bit happier, and if my father could have been like Mr Karimi, paying more attention to my mother and loving us more, surely I would have been able to talk by now.

The days passed by without incident. No one spoke of my going to school any more. Mr and Mrs Karimi came and took me out a few times. I was comfortable around them. They loved me just the way I was and didn't expect anything from me. Each time after I got home I would mull over these outings for several hours. But they soon came to an end. Father's coolness towards them showed that he wasn't happy about my relationship with them. I missed them and felt that Father's role in our separation was another sign of his enmity towards me.

On one of the final days of the year Mrs Karimi called and asked Mother if they could come over. Father argued with Mother for a while asking why she hadn't come up with an excuse. When they arrived he greeted them coldly. To make up for his lack of affection I opened my arms and embraced Mr Karimi. I theatrically kissed his cheek and held on to him tightly as Father looked on angrily. Father was cross and this made me happy. They had brought me a big walking robot. I felt proud. For the first time I was the one receiving attention. Just me. I hugged the robot and stroked it.

Father said meanly, 'He smashes whatever we get for him. Be careful you don't break this one!'

Asi said, 'He's so stupid! We like this and won't break it. We only break the toys he gets us when he wants to fool us. We ruin those to annoy him. But we won't break the Karimis' toy because they love us.'

I was so happy I didn't realize they were there to say goodbye. They were going abroad to visit their children and it wasn't clear if I would ever see them again.

CHAPTER 33

The New Year was a glorious event. Mother seemed happier the closer it got. She laughed more and seemed less tired. Her joy brightened the entire house. Our problems seemed less important, there were fewer arguments and a sense of excitement took us over. Mother would gather all the savings she'd hidden away here and there, and visit the bank. She bought us new clothes and gifts that she wrapped and hid away in suitcases like precious secrets, careful to keep them from breaking or wrinkling. She didn't even show them to Father. The happy event we'd all anticipated for an entire year would take place over the New Year holidays; the day when Father would come home holding train tickets, and Mother would scream with joy. We would circle around her jumping up and down, and laughing excitedly. Once we knew the exact date of our trip the countdown would begin. It was like magic. Time would fly by faster and things would happen more quickly.

My heart beat with happiness when we finally went to the train station. This long iron snake was the most beautiful, powerful thing in the world to me. Strange sounds and smells hovered magically around it. I observed all its details carefully, even bending down to look underneath. The oily rails and the gravel between them made me dizzy, and I would shudder imagining what it would be like to fall down there. I wanted to touch the train and become one with it, travelling to faraway lands in the belly of this magnificent creature. The most exciting time was when the whistle blew and the train began to rumble and shake. I would move myself closer to the window and look out as the train sped away. Everything was interesting.

After hurrying about for the past hour, trying to get everything done, Father would finally begin to calm down. His anxiety was replaced with a wan sort of happiness. He would drop down on his seat, give a brief smile and ask Mother, 'So what have we got to eat?' This was one of the rare moments when Father became talkative. He would tell Arash about the stations, the way the train worked, the number of tunnels and the train's timetable. I found this information interesting too and listened carefully. I heard and memorized it all, but I didn't want him to know I found what he said interesting, because he wasn't saying it to me. So I would pretend to do something else. I never forgot the rules of combat I'd devised.

The South was always warm and lovely. The air smelled of kindness. To be loved here you didn't need to speak or be smart and flawless; just being a grandchild was enough. Everyone would hug you and introduce you to others with pride. Gazes were gentle and kind, and words were filled with love. Grandmother was called Bibi. Unlike my other grandmother, she wasn't afraid to hug her grandchildren and shower them with love. She laughingly and loudly expressed her love for us and wasn't worried that it would lower her authority. She would give us the presents she'd bought for us over the year. We would eat large delicious lotuses out of sight of Father because he believed they caused stomachaches, and we would play under the shade of large green trees amidst the scent of orange blossoms. There were always many people around. We would go from house to house, and everyone we met added to our happiness. In those days it felt as if this part of Iran was in a constant state of celebration; that everyone here was always on holiday.

Mother became talkative. She talked of everything as if she'd held it all in for a whole year to unleash in two weeks. Even Father, in all his seriousness, couldn't ignore this level of affection and hospitality. He spoke to my uncles and laughed at their jokes. I felt lighter in this place. It didn't upset me that I couldn't talk. They understood me, and my lack of speech became so unimportant that it was no longer a burden to me. I wouldn't feel sick or be filled with fear every time I thought about it. I knew no one would make fun of me. I would begin to whisper some words. But time was too short; before I was ready to speak the trip would be over and we would return to our sad, silent life.

The first few days after coming back were the most depressing. Mother would sigh and listen to music from the South, going deeper and deeper into her own shell. She wasn't going to get used to being away from her birthplace. And Father, who was the reason for her being away from home, was no help. Her soul, happiness and conversation had been left behind. Here she had nothing but loneliness and a sense of alienation.

Father would get busy with work again. Conversations in our house felt cold and distant, and did not inspire me to talk. I wondered why Arash's father and his family didn't know kind, affectionate speech. If he talked to Mother more, if he used words like 'dear', 'sweetheart' or 'darling', maybe she wouldn't be so sad. Maybe then I would be able to talk too.

Asi said, 'He knows how to do it. He used to call her these things before. That's why she married him. But now he doesn't want to say them any longer.'

Babi asked, 'But why?'

'Because of us. Because Mother has a son like us.'

Arash would go back to his books and his various classes again. The poor boy had no choice but to excel at school. He had to be a genius to make up for Father's embarrassment over having a retarded child. Arash's childhood had been lost under this heavy burden, and now he wanted to take away his teenage years too. Arash was slowly forgetting how to laugh and be happy.

Shadi was the only happy person around. She did whatever she wanted and no one expected anything from her. She could play, laugh, and be a normal, healthy child.

I didn't need to speak in such a house. All the joyful self-expression I'd developed during those two weeks in the South simply disappeared.

CHAPTER 34

A phone call in mid-spring brought chaos into our lives. Mother cried out like she'd gone mad. Fataneh and Fereshteh came over and gave her sugar water. Father came home early but Mother didn't stop crying.

'My father is ill! I have to go home!'

Father took her hand and said, 'Okay, okay. Try to stay calm in front of the children. Fereshteh, can you please take the kids over to your house?'

I ran and hung on to Mother's legs, but she didn't even notice me. Father took my hand and placed it in Fereshteh's. Fataneh picked Shadi up and we all went to Uncle's house.

Everyone talked in whispers at Uncle's house. I stood in a corner and carefully listened to what they said, observing every move they made. Fereshteh said, 'Are you sure? Maryam just said he was ill.'

'That's what they told her, but they called Nasser at work and said it was over.'

'Poor Maryam! She's going to go there hopeful, and once she gets there she'll realize it's all over. She loved her father.'

Asi said, 'Did you hear that? Grandfather is over.'

I imagined his kind face. When we were in the South he'd take us out every day and buy us ice cream.

Babi said, 'Do you know what it means to be over? It means he's dead.'

I could imagine 'being over' better than I could understand 'being dead'. Something that was over could begin again. I was deep in thought.

Asi said, 'Mother's going to go there. We'll get on the train again!'

The joy of going back to that land of kindness pushed aside the sorrow of Grandfather being over, or being dead, which I couldn't fully comprehend. I just couldn't understand why they'd sent me over to Uncle's house.

Babi said, 'Remember to take some of the chocolate bars Mother hid in the fridge for our cousins.'

I left Uncle's house and headed back home. I kept thinking about the word 'dead', which made me anxious in an unfamiliar way.

Babi said, 'Remember how Mother used to say dying is like going to sleep for a long time? How long do you think it'll be?'

Asi replied, 'A long time. It's not like how *we* sleep. He has to go to sleep in a special place.'

'Like where?'

'I think somewhere like a hospital.'

'Can we visit him?'

'I don't know!'

When I got home the door was locked. I couldn't reach the door-bell. I slammed on the door with my fists. Mother always recognized the sound of my knocks and opened the door immediately. But this time no one opened the door. I kicked it, then lay on the ground and peeked under the garage door. I couldn't see the tyres of Father's car. Where had they gone? Mother usually didn't go out without me in the mornings. My throat felt restricted. I kicked at the front door again, angry and tearful. Fereshteh rushed out of their house. The buttons of her coat were undone and she hadn't tied on her scarf properly. She ran towards me and picked me up.

'Shahaab, darling, why did you leave without permission?

149

Let's go.' I pulled my hand away. 'There's no one here. Your father's taken your mother somewhere, but he'll be right back. Let's go. Would you like to go to the amusement park? I'll take you this afternoon. Remember how we went last year and you rode the Ferris wheel? Your dad will be back home by the time we get back from the park. You'll sleep in your own bed tonight. I promise.'

I calmed down a bit. There was nothing else I could do so I let Fereshteh take me back to Uncle's house.

Shadi played with Fataneh without a care in the world, but I couldn't let go of the thought of the strange thing Mother had done. Didn't she want to see her father? So where had she gone now? She had to pack our suitcases and set aside travelling clothes for us. Babi said, 'Maybe she's gone to buy presents.' Mother usually started buying gifts a month before our New Year trip. I always thought of these as special prizes, and unlike my usual objections to shopping, I enjoyed this process and found it exciting.

That afternoon Uncle took us to the amusement park. We got on many rides, but I was distracted and felt anxious. On the way back, Shadi fell asleep in Fataneh's arms. Fataneh took off her shoes and put her in her own bed, which surprised me. Fereshteh took my hand and said, 'Let's go home. Your father's back by now.'

I pulled my hand away and tried to wake Shadi up to take her home with me. Fataneh got upset and said, 'Stop it, you'll wake her up!'

But Fereshteh understood me and said, 'Don't worry, Shahaab. Shadi will stay here tonight.' I shook my head and tried to go towards Shadi again. Fereshteh pulled my hand. 'Your mother asked us to keep Shadi here as long as she's away.'

I looked at her in fear. As long as she's away? Aren't we taking Shadi with us to visit Grandfather? Why would mother do such a cruel thing to Shadi? My thoughts were confused. I ran home. Uncle and Fereshteh followed me there. Arash opened the door with the first knock. Father's car was there. I ran towards the house, side-stepping Father's outstretched arms. I looked in the hall, the kitchen and Arash's room downstairs. Then I hurried upstairs. I opened Mother's door. The lights were on. Clothes were strewn on the bed and the wardrobe door was ajar, but there was no sign of Mother. What did it mean? I looked in the bathroom but she wasn't there either. I was gripped with fear. What if she was gone? Was it possible she'd left without me? I went back outside.

Father, Uncle, Fereshteh and Arash were sitting on a bench in the garden.

Father said, 'We were lucky. We couldn't find a ticket. All the flights were booked. But I suddenly ran into Hesam Hazrati, remember our neighbour in Amiriyeh? I'm not sure what he does at the airport, but he was a godsend. He went and found us a ticket as soon as he heard the story. She finally flew out two hours ago. I asked her to call as soon as she arrived. She was very worried about the kids, especially Shahaab. She thinks I won't be able to handle him.'

I couldn't believe it. So Mother had gone and left me with Arash's father? Was this really possible? Fereshteh turned around and saw me.

'Shahaab, sweetheart, come here. Your mother will be back soon. She had to go because her father's ill, but she'll bring you lots of presents when she comes back.'

I shut the front door with all my might and ran up the stairs to my room. What betrayal! Mother had gone away and left me with Arash's father! Didn't she remember he'd tried to send me away to school? Didn't she know he hadn't even searched for me when I was lost, that it was because of Mr Karimi that I'd been found? And when they finally found me everyone was happy except for him. He'd gone and argued with the police instead! I felt alone in the whole wide world. I hid under the covers still wearing my shoes and clothes. Father came upstairs and opened the door. I turned to the wall and shut my eyes tight. He pulled aside the covers, sat on the edge of the bed, and took off my shoes and socks and put them aside. If Mother were here she would give me a kiss on the cheek too. At that moment I really needed that kiss, even if it from was Arash's father.

Arash came in and said, 'He fell asleep quickly!'

'He's a child. He's lucky he doesn't understand anything. He was too tired. He's been out all day and even went to the amusement park. Your uncle said he's already had supper.'

'But he's still wearing his clothes and hasn't brushed his teeth. Mother would never let him go to sleep like that.'

'Let him be. Nothing will happen if he sleeps like this for a night. I'm very tired myself. I have so much to do tomorrow. You should go to bed too. You have school tomorrow.'

'What are we going to do about him?'

'Drop him off at your uncle's before you leave in the morning.'

They turned off the lights, shut the door, and left. I pulled the blanket aside. The room was so dark. Father had forgotten to turn on my nightlight. Asi said, 'He doesn't care if we die of fright in this dark room. Or if all our teeth rot and fall out. Or if we sleep with dirty clothes on and get ill. It'll make him happy.'

I missed Mother terribly. Even though I was angry and couldn't forgive her for leaving me, I still loved her with all my heart and knew she loved me too. I wiped my tears and pressed my face in the pillow so no one would hear me crying.

I spent the next day at Uncle's house, bored with nothing to do. I couldn't stop thinking of Mother. Why didn't she take us with her? I had been a good boy and hadn't broken anything but she'd left me behind. Father picked us up in the evening and took us home. He fried a few eggs that were runny on top and burnt on the bottom. I didn't touch them. He said, 'Shahaab, why won't you eat? Go on.' I lowered my head. 'Do you want something else?' I looked at him with surprise. He was being kind. 'What do you want? Tell me and I'll get it for you.' I was disappointed. 'From now on, everyone needs to tell me if they need anything. Like this: "Arash, what would you like?"'

'Some bread.'

'Here you go. Shadi, what do you want?'

'Water.'

152

'Here you are. Shahaab, what do you want? Tell me and I'll give you whatever you want.'

Different thoughts ran through my mind. Asi said, 'He wants to kill us from hunger and thirst. He knows we can't talk!' I got up angrily. The chair fell back. I ran up the stairs, shut the door and calmed down.

From that day on we were openly at war. The more he tried to make me talk, the more I resisted. He said, 'Tell me what you want and I'll buy it for you. I'll do whatever you want. Just tell me.'

I would ignore my wants, become angry and keep silent.

Asi said, 'He can buy us anything, but he won't because we can't talk.'

The issue of talking became more and more important, and increased my terror and anxiety. On the fourth night Mother was away, Father took us to a fast-food joint that had recently opened in the neighbourhood. I loved hamburgers. He praised the food there for a while and then said, 'Each of you tell me what you want. Arash, what would you like?'

'A burger.'

'Shadi, what about you?'

'Burder.'

'Very good.' My heart was beating fast. I was hungry and the delicious smell of grilled hamburgers increased my appetite. 'Shahaab, darling, what would you like?' I looked at him in disbelief. Had he really brought me here to witness the others eat and stay hungry? 'Tell me, son, just say one word: "ham-bur-ger". They're really delicious.' I was on the verge of tears and angrily turned my back to him. Watching the people around me eating with gusto had made me very hungry. 'Just say "ham" and I'll know what you're trying to say. I'll get it for you.'

I pursed my lips. Babi said, 'He's right. Give him a sign so he'll know what you like. See how delicious it is. Hurry up, I'm really hungry.'

With some hesitation I pointed at the kid sitting at the next table. Father tried to remain calm but his voice was beginning to shake.

'No, this won't do. You can speak, I know it. Open your mouth and say something. Sign language is not acceptable.'

Arash stepped in. 'Didn't you hear him? Shahaab just said "hamburger", but he said it in a quiet voice. I heard him. Get him a burger too.'

'No, he has to say it loud enough for me to hear.'

Asi said, 'Arash feels sorry for us too, but *he* doesn't. We'll never talk to him even if we starve to death!'

These actions made speaking that much more difficult for me. Father would inexpertly put himself in a spot. He couldn't bear to keep me hungry but he couldn't go back on the demand he'd made either. He got up annoyed and ordered our food. Upset with his own failure, he threw a burger in front of me and said, 'Eat!'

My throat felt tight. With tearful eyes I swallowed the burger with difficulty.

At the weekend Father said he was taking us on a walk at a large park in the mountains with some of his friends from work. Fereshteh took Shadi to their house, bathed and dressed her, and tied her hair with yellow ribbons. Arash bathed and dressed himself. Father had to take me to shower with him. He washed my hair fast. I remembered when I used to bathe with Mr Karimi. We would play and laugh. Bathing with Mother was pleasant too. It felt like her hands were caressing me as she washed me. She would kiss my neck when I was cleaned up and say, 'Yummy! Clean kisses are so delicious.'

I missed her. I needed her kind hands and her gentle kisses so badly.

The park was big and beautiful. The new leaves had a fresh greenness to them. Some of the trees had turned crimson. The yellow, bright light of the sun was pleasantly warm. The scent of violets and jasmine filled the air, and absorbed in all these colours I took deep breaths, smelling the fresh spring air. We met Father's friends at a large pool in the park: three men, a woman and five kids of differing ages. The men seemed close to Father but were also very respectful towards him. One of them automatically said, 'Yes, boss,' and I realized Father must be their superior at the office.

Father proudly introduced Arash, 'This is Arash. I've told you about him before. He's first in his class, a straight-A student. You'll soon see his name among the winners of the maths and physics Olympiad. And this is Shadi, our chatterbox. She's three and a half.' I stayed in a corner, curious to see what he was going to say about me. Father looked around. 'There's also Shahaab.' Like saying: 'We also have a dog.' 'He's around here somewhere.' I was sure he knew I was standing behind him, but he didn't turn around. 'So, Abedi, which of these are yours?'

I didn't hear the rest of their conversation. I separated from the group. The woman who was married to one of the men came over and said, 'Why didn't your mother come along?' I shrugged my shoulders and ran away.

We all started walking. Arash hooked up with two older boys his own age, but he acted as if he was superior to them. With her childish patter Shadi soon received the attention of the woman accompanying us. Father started to talk of work. I was forgotten and followed them from a short distance. I missed Mother. After a while I felt I needed to go to the loo. In all this time Father hadn't ever asked if I needed to use the loo. We'd left home in such a rush in the morning that I'd forgotten to go then. I didn't know what to do. My stomach was rumbling and I felt a great pressure inside. I resisted and the pressure became less. But after a few steps it increased and I couldn't stand still any longer. I ran to Father, took his hand, and looked at him the way I looked at Mother at these times. Mother would immediately understand, but Father looked at me surprised and continued his conversation. I pulled on his hand and he angrily pulled it back.

'What is it? What do you want? Go and play with the others.'

I put my hand on my stomach and looked at him pleadingly. A fat boy that was walking along with his father said, 'I'm hungry too. We've walked a long way.'

His father said, 'I'll get some cakes and drinks from the stand there.'

The pressure was greater now, my eyes burned and there was a whistling sound in my ears. I stomped my feet and placed my hand on my stomach. Father was busy talking. The man came back with the cakes and drinks, and handed me a cake. The pressure was unbearable. I couldn't understand why grown-ups were so stupid. I threw the cake away and everyone stared at me, surprised. Father gave me a mean look and pressed his lips together. He took my arm and pressed it and said in a low voice so the others wouldn't hear, 'What is it again, you idiot? Are you trying to embarrass me?'

He was so afraid of embarrassment. He was pointlessly showing off in front of his colleagues. I released my tensed muscles. A warm liquid slid down my legs and dripped out of my trousers. An unpleasant smell filled the air. My trousers had turned heavy. Everyone looked at me. Father first turned pale and then red. The woman said, 'Oh my God! He's soiled himself!'

Father was so flustered he didn't know what to do. He collected himself but couldn't calm down. He pulled on my hand with hatred. The woman pointed to the toilets. We left a dirty, smelly trail behind us. Everyone who passed by frowned and pinched their nose, looking at us strangely.

Father poured some water on my legs. He was unwilling to touch me, and kept cursing. He smacked my head several times. He was about to explode with anger, but I felt a strange calmness. I had been physically and emotionally emptied.

CHAPTER 35

My painful trip finally came to an end. For the first time, I was eager to return home. Thoughts of my children hadn't left me for even a moment. Despite my deep heartfelt pain I hadn't been able to grieve properly. Since I was the deceased's only daughter I'd had to help my mother with all the mourners and I'd been unable to express my own feelings of sadness with so much to do. The only place I wanted to be now was home.

Arash and Shadi came to greet me happily, but Shahaab ran and hid in his room. Nasser said, 'Nothing he does is normal! He gave me a really hard time.'

I knew his behaviour was a type of protest. I followed him upstairs and pulled him out from behind his bed. I knew all his tricks. He was trying to show he was upset with me, but when I hugged him tight and kissed him, he let go of all his resistance and fell into my arms.

I tried to turn everything back to normal as soon as possible. I did the daily tasks that I never enjoyed doing. But no matter how hard I tried, my heartache wouldn't stop. I spoke to my mother and brothers every day on the phone, and cried. Shahaab carefully observed me all the time, but Nasser didn't pay any attention to my mental state. He worked as hard as ever and came home late every night. He would point out the self-sacrifices he made for the sake of his family. He constantly talked of the hard time he'd had when I'd been away, when he'd had to work and take care of the kids at the same time. I didn't want to argue with him, to point out it was his responsibility, but I couldn't bear his sense of indebtedness either. He wouldn't get tired of describing the episode in the park, each time telling the story with more anger and shame. I was surprised the first time I heard the story.

'I can't believe it. How could Shahaab do such a thing?'

'Well, he did! He stood in front of my colleagues and their children, looked me in the eyes and shamelessly shat himself! You can't imagine how I felt.'

'He must have been sick. Maybe he ate something bad and couldn't help himself.'

'No, there was nothing wrong with him!'

'Then maybe he didn't use the loo in the morning – you know it usually takes him a long time in the mornings. You have to be patient. Sometimes he even takes his toys and plays with them in the bathroom.'

'And you won't believe me when I tell you he's crazy! He plays with his toys in the bathroom?'

'Stop it! He's a child. Don't make such a big deal out of everything. It happens to everyone. Your colleagues have kids too, they'll understand.'

'I can't even hold my head up in the office any longer. Do you think they have any respect for a boss who has to wipe his child's shitty arse?'

'You're making a fuss. What do you expect from me anyway? Do you want me to get rid of him?'

'No, spoil him as usual! He did it on purpose just to annoy me. You should have seen the look he gave me – it was mean, stubborn and victorious.'

'Why would he give you a mean, stubborn look? Did you do anything to him?'

'I gave him a bath and put clean clothes on him. I made him eggs for breakfast and took him to the park. I even treated them to a restaurant. And that is how he repaid me!'

Forty days later I had to go away again for a couple of days to attend a memorial service for my father. I sat Shahaab down and explained why I needed to leave and how long I would be gone. Contrary to what I'd expected, he understood why I had to go and accepted it.

CHAPTER 36

Mother didn't trick me this time. She explained everything before she left, so her absence wasn't as painful. When she returned home with Bibi, I ran with everyone else to greet them.

Bibi's presence was a strange occurrence in our lives. We were always the ones who went over to her house – I couldn't remember her ever coming over to ours. Her appearance, the clothes she wore, her scarf and the way she talked, which all seemed so pleasant and agreeable in her own town, seemed out of place in the city, and Bibi herself was aware of this more than anyone else. She'd somehow lost her self-confidence. This strong woman, who ordered everyone around in her own setting, became shy in ours. When Grandmother, with all her airs, came to visit Bibi along with my aunts and Fataneh, she turned even shyer, especially since Grandmother made biting remarks about her scarf, and the addition to our household expenses.

Asi said, 'I wish we had another brick to drop on her head.'

For the first time in his life Father said something right, 'Bibi's honoured us with her presence. She is so kind to us whenever we go over to her house. I hope she'll consider this her own home and stay with us for as long as she can.'

Bibi lowered her head and said, 'Thank you, son, but I'm more comfortable in my own house. Maryam insisted that I come this time. I told her there are good doctors in my own town, but she wouldn't hear of it. She said I had to come to Tehran to see a specialist. I have an appointment on Monday, so I would appreciate it if you could get me a return ticket for Tuesday.'

Mother said, 'What? I didn't go through all this trouble so you'd go back as soon as you arrived. No way! You're going to spend the summer with us. Furthermore, the doctor is going to require all sorts of tests and X-rays, so you'll have to wait until they're all done. You can't leave so soon, I want you to stay!'

And so Bibi came to stay with us for a while. She went with Mother to see various doctors and do tests several times a week. At other times she was an invisible presence on the periphery of our lives. She seemed depressed and lonely. This wasn't the Bibi I knew. Whenever Mother found some time, she would sit next to her and they would talk about Grandfather, shedding tears. She occupied the corners of our house and I would sometimes forget she was even there.

After the park incident, Father and I had become blatantly hostile. We trod carefully around each other, like two opponents expecting an attack from the enemy. One day he came home and said, 'Our CEO, Mr Arbabi, is back from Mecca and he's invited everyone over for a garden party at the weekend. He's going to serve kebabs.' He turned to Mother and quietly continued, 'He'll probably announce my promotion that day.'

Asi said, 'Yummy! Kebabs!' I swallowed, and enthusiastically waited for the weekend.

Mother and I spent three days looking for a suitable gift for Mr Arbabi. Finally, we both chose a beautiful, expensive serving dish. I proudly held it all the way home. I couldn't wait for the weekend to arrive. Firstly, because we didn't get invited to garden parties very often, and secondly, because I wanted to be on my best behaviour and show Mother that I was a good boy and that the park incident Father kept harping on about had not been my fault.

I woke up earlier than usual on the anticipated day. I washed my face and put on a pair of shorts and a khaki T-shirt Mother had recently bought for me. I combed my hair and went downstairs. The others weren't at breakfast yet. Bibi was the only one in the kitchen. She looked at me with surprise and said, 'What a handsome little boy! You get the top mark today because you're the first one ready.' I smiled. 'You must be very excited about the garden party.' I ate my breakfast with appetite. When Mother saw the table all laid she said, 'Bibi, you shouldn't have. Thanks so much. We all slept in today and we're rather late.'

Bibi looked at me with a smile and said, 'Except for my blond boy here. He's been up since dawn. He's washed himself, had breakfast, used the loo and is waiting for you. See how handsome he looks.'

The kitchen got crowded when Shadi and Father arrived. Mother called Arash. She poured tea for everyone and they all began eating breakfast. Father said, 'Hurry up and get ready. We're supposed to meet the others on the road at ten.'

I went into the hall and sat in front of the TV. I felt calm and superior because I was ready before any of them. They were all running around. Arash was looking for his shirt and yelled, 'Mother, where's my blue shirt?'

'Wear something else.'

'No, I want to wear that one.'

'It was dirty, I put it in the laundry basket.'

Eventually they all got ready. Shadi wore a red shirt with white leggings and her hair was in a ponytail. Arash came downstairs grumbling. Father took the car out of the garage and came back into the house to pick up a bag he'd left behind. We hurried to the car. I sat next to the window. I felt it was my right because I'd been ready before anyone else. At the front door Mother told Bibi, 'I'm so sorry. We'll try to get back early. There's food in the fridge.' Bibi lifted her arm and waved at us. Father got to the car and took a look inside before getting behind the wheel. He suddenly froze in place as if he'd had an electric shock.

He protested, 'Where do you think you're going?', and he angrily walked towards Mother who was still talking to Bibi.

'Maryam, where's he going? Weren't you going to send him to his uncle's?'

I looked on in disbelief. I knew he was my enemy, but I hadn't realized to what extent.

'It's not fair. Let him come. He won't disturb you.'

'No way! I told you before. I am not comfortable with these people; everyone's going to be there. It's an important day for me. If he makes a mess or embarrasses me in any way I won't be able to hold my head high in front of them any more.'

'He's all dressed and ready to go – we can't leave him. I'll watch him all the time.'

'No! I told you from the start. You were supposed to make plans for him. You didn't do it on purpose so I wouldn't have a choice. But there's no way in hell that I'm taking him along. I don't feel comfortable around him. He embarrasses me. I have to keep explaining why he won't talk, why he's dumb, etc. I don't want people to look at me with pity or try to discover my weakness.'

'What are you talking about? What weakness?'

'You don't know how things are at the office. A while back Kermani – the janitor, who's now a member of the Islamic Association and pretty much involved in everything – said, "Those who don't believe in God and the prophet Mohammad have retarded children." The way things are in the country now, and at the office in particular, I don't want to be labelled a non-believer.'

'What an idiot! Only a sick mind can come up with these ideas. Why did you even listen to him? Instead of smacking him in the mouth you actually paid attention to what he said?'

'I don't agree with him, but they're in charge now and my position at work may be jeopardized.'

All my excitement was replaced with a painful sense of dejection. With the little pride I had left, I got out of the car and walked inside. The pressure of this humiliation was too much to bear. They continued to argue for a bit longer, but I went to my room, lay on the bed and stared at the ceiling. I still had a tiny bit of hope left. They came upstairs after a few moments.

Babi said, 'See, she's here! Mother won't leave us alone.'

She sat on the bed, stroked my head and said, 'Shahaab, darling, I'll take you to the park tomorrow and we'll get pizza for lunch. I promise. And next week we'll all go on a picnic with Bibi, won't we, Nasser? You promised.'

'Yes, next week we'll go to the park with Bibi, I promise. Maryam, I'm going to buy him a bike too!'

'Really? Good for him!'

'Yes, a red bike. Now be a good boy and stay with Bibi, we'll be back soon.'

Mother kissed my cheek. 'Don't be sad, dear. You'll go and buy a bike with your father tomorrow. You're lucky; I wish I didn't have to go today! I don't feel like hanging out with these people. You'd get bored if you came with us.'

'Maryam, let's go, it's getting late.'

Mother got off the bed, looked at me sadly and left. I hated her. Why didn't she stand up for me? She was so weak. The sound of the car shattered any remaining shreds of hope I had. I ran to the window and saw it as it turned the corner and disappeared. They didn't take me! I still couldn't believe it. I clenched my teeth with anger, and wiped my tears with the backs of my hands.

Asi said, 'To hell with red bikes!'

I was going crazy. I went to my parents' bedroom but the door was locked. I kicked and punched the door, but it was useless. Bibi limped up the stairs and took me down with her. She constantly talked and told me stories, but I couldn't even hear a word she said. Black thoughts of revenge circled in my mind. What could I do that would match how they'd treated me?

Asi said, 'I'll kill them! Just wait and see.'

Babi cried, 'How? We're so much weaker than they are. We can't do anything.'

'Yes, we can. We're not weaker than Shadi. They'll be very sorry if we kill Shadi. We'll take her on the roof and push her off.'

'But Shadi isn't here now.'

'We'll burn their house down. It's easy. We'll light a match like Khosrow and throw it in a wardrobe.'

'But nothing will happen to them.'

'We'll burn it down when they're asleep. Yes, fire's a good idea!'

I spent the rest of the morning inconsolable and furious, plotting my revenge in my room. I couldn't be around anyone, not even Bibi, and she left me alone. At lunch-time she called me to come and eat with her, and warmed up the cutlets from the night before. She laid them on the table with yoghurt, vegetables and bread.

I was still undecided between two options: in my mind sometimes I burned my family to death, and sometimes I watched Shadi fall from the rooftop to the ground. At the time, Shadi seemed like my parents' favourite doll, which I was destroying to take revenge on them. So when I imagined her bloodied, broken corpse on the ground, I not only didn't feel any regret or remorse, but also worried that their lovable idol might not be completely broken.

Asi said, 'If she's still okay after she falls, we'll cut off her head with a knife.'

Bibi kept pleading with me to eat a few mouthfuls. The food seemed so tasteless and dry. It surprised me because I'd found it so delicious the night before. I imagined the beautiful garden party and the delicious food they were having. I could smell the mouth-watering kebabs. I saw Shadi eating a large piece of kebab. I threw my plate of cutlets on the floor and spat out the dry food in my mouth.

Bibi got up and walked towards me. I was gripping the fork tightly, ready to kill her too. A great desire for destruction had filled my entire body. Contrary to what I'd expected, Bibi didn't tell me off. She sat across from me, covered her eyes with her scarf and began to cry out loud. In between her sobbing she said, 'I'm so sorry for you, child. I wish I were dead and hadn't witnessed how these ruthless people mistreated you. You have a right to be angry. I'd be angry too if I were you.'

I was shocked. I looked at her with surprise. No one had

allowed me to be angry or violent before. My hand went limp and I dropped the fork. With the sound of the fork dropping Bibi took her hands away from her eyes. She took my hand and pulled me into her arms. Her shoulders still shook with her sobs. I pressed my head against her chest. It smelled of rose water and warm pastries. I gave in to her embrace and let out the sadness I'd been feeling all day. She stroked my head with her kind hands and let me cry.

After a while she said, 'Shahaab, you're a very good boy. Nothing is wrong with you. In my opinion you're smarter than the whole lot of them, but they're too stupid to realize it. If I were you I wouldn't talk to them either.' She started to cry again. 'If you want to break anything, go ahead, I'll help you.'

I was startled. I hesitantly picked up a glass and dropped it on the floor. Bibi picked up her own glass and dropped it too. I felt thrilled. I looked around and took some plates from the dish-rack and threw them on the floor. Bibi picked up her plate, which still had some cutlets and yoghurt on it and threw it on the floor. Yoghurt spread all over the place. I couldn't believe it! I started to laugh.

Bibi said, 'You know what? These things only affect your mother. Breaking her things doesn't satisfy me. I want to break something of your father's.' It felt as if someone else was speaking my mind. I eagerly nodded my head, took Bibi's hand and dragged her up the stairs. She limped up but didn't protest. I stood outside the door to my parents' room.

Bibi said, 'It's no use, they've locked the door.'

I pointed above the door. I could see the key up there. I jumped several times but couldn't reach it. Bibi stretched her arm too but it was useless. I ran into my room and brought a small stool. Bibi climbed up on to the stool with some difficulty, but still couldn't reach the key. She fell as she was trying to come down. I ran to her, worried. She pulled my hand and embraced me and laughed. 'Look at us, like a couple of madmen.' We hugged each other and laughed some more. The pain and hatred inside me vanished for a few moments. Bibi said, 'Is this your room? I wanted to share your room, but since my leg hurts, your mother put my things in Arash's room downstairs. Do you want to show me your room?' I helped her get up and took her to my room. She looked around and said, 'What a pleasant room. I want to stay here. Will you share your room with me?' I nodded with enthusiasm. 'Then let's bring up my things.' I remembered her painful leg and pointed to her knee.

She said, 'Don't worry. If you help me when I go up and down the stairs it won't hurt as much. Will you help me?' I nodded several times. We limped down the stairs together and brought up Bibi's essential things. I wanted to bring her suitcase too but she said, 'I don't need that. We'll just take whatever I need from it. So what do you think we should do now? Should we clean the kitchen and have a nap, or leave it as it is?'

I started to think. I didn't feel like continuing the fight any more. I don't know what had happened, but it wasn't as important to me. I shrugged my shoulders.

Bibi said, 'I won't clean up everything, but let's pick up the broken glass so it doesn't go into our feet, okay? Will you help too so it gets done quicker? Then we can have a nap and I'll tell you a story.'

We cleaned the kitchen together. Then Bibi climbed up the stairs with my help. She spread a blanket on the floor and put our pillows next to each other. I put my head on her arm. I really loved this closeness. Shadi always slept next to Mother like this. There had been no room in Mother's arms for me ever since Shadi had arrived. I cuddled next to Bibi and listened to her melodic voice, and soon fell asleep.

CHAPTER 37

'Climbing up and down stairs isn't good for you. If you're not comfortable in Arash's room I'll send him upstairs and you can have the room to yourself.'

'No! I want to stay in Shahaab's room.'

Nasser continued, 'Apart from the stairs, he won't be able to help you if you need anything because he doesn't understand anything and can't talk.'

My mother angrily replied, 'He understands everything! What troubles me here isn't the stairs!' And she turned away. I looked at Nasser with surprise.

After he left for work I asked Mother, 'Why are you so upset? Nasser didn't mean anything. He only has your well-being in mind.'

She shook her head sadly and said, 'What can I say? You people don't realize the things you say. I'm very worried about you. It's as if you don't understand at all.'

'Understand what?'

'This child, Arash, each other. You call this a life? All your schooling seems to have been for nothing!'

I didn't understand what she meant. Dismayed, I asked, 'What happened? What upset you?'

'Everything! I've been here for three weeks now. Something

seems to be missing from this house wherever I look. It's as if you're all on bad terms with each other; everyone stays in their own corner doing their own thing. There's no sign of humour, of playfulness. No one's told a joke or laughed out loud in all the time I've been here. What kind of a husband and wife are you? You never even talk to each other. You do housework all day with a frown on your face, which scares even me, let alone your children. Why are you so sad?'

'I'm not sad, but I don't like housework. It makes me feel useless. I have all these degrees but in the end I'm just a plain housewife, like a woman from the past century.'

'So what? You're doing it for your children. Just because you've gone to university doesn't mean your kids should starve.'

'Am I not doing enough here? I work day and night, washing, cleaning and cooking for them, disregarding my own wants and desires. And in the end you call me a bad mother and disapprove of my life!'

'Of course I don't approve. Everything you do with a frown on your face, nagging and grumbling, is like poison for your children. All you're doing here is meeting your responsibilities. Big deal! Just because you've studied doesn't mean you don't need to cook and clean after your kids.'

'I only meant that this is not *all* I want to do.'

'Well, do more if you can. But if you can't, then at least meet your responsibilities properly. Whatever one does out of love is less difficult and tiring. And that husband of yours; it's as if he's the only man in the world who works! Whenever he comes home he acts as if he's moved mountains!'

'He's tired, Mother. He works three jobs.'

'He should quit if he can't handle it. The two of you have made mountains out of molehills, making a big deal of all you have to do. This isn't good for your children. You should think of them more.'

'It's worrying about the children that's killing us!'

'Stop coming up with excuses. There's nothing wrong with your children. You're the problem here. Ill-tempered parents will have ill-tempered children. If you fix yourselves the kids will turn out fine.'

'Do you think it's our fault that Shahaab's the way he is?'

'What way? There's nothing wrong with him. If anyone labels this child ill one more time, I'll let them have it!'

I looked at her, standing before me like a lioness, with awe. Unlike most times, when the slightest remark would annoy me, her speech hadn't upset me at all.

CHAPTER 38

Bibi became my room-mate. For the first time there was someone around who accepted all my shortcomings. My lack of speech was not an issue for Bibi and didn't keep us from communicating. My room became our special world, where we had a pleasant sense of security when we shut the door. Bibi didn't insist on making me talk. I wasn't scared with her, and didn't feel the anxiety of having to pass a test. One night as I was sleeping next to her, listening to one of her enchanting tales, she said, 'I can tell you the rest tomorrow night if you're too sleepy.'

I shook my head. She asked again, and I shook my head once more. Bibi said, 'I can't see your head in the dark, sweetheart. Either touch me on the hand, or make a sound. If you want to say yes, just say 'ahem', like you're clearing your throat. And if you want to say no, make another sound, like the beeping of a car for instance. Do you want me to continue the story?'

I touched her hand and said, 'Ahem.'

Bibi continued the story. It was about a boy who was put under a spell, and couldn't talk. But the brave boy found the key to the spell and set everyone free. I liked the story very much. I wanted Bibi to tell it over and over again. But sometimes it seemed as if she'd forgotten it.

The next afternoon at nap time I went into her arms, hugged

her and showed that I was ready for a story. She began a different one. I shook my head in protest. Bibi said, 'Which one do you want? I can't tell which story you want me to tell. Can you give me a small hint?'

I stuttered, 'Sp ... Spe ... Spell ...'

'Oh, the story of the witch who casts a spell to keep the little boy from talking?'

I happily replied, 'Aha.'

Bibi, acting quite naturally, told the story, as if nothing special had happened. That night she asked, 'Which story do you want now?'

Less anxiously than at noon I said, 'The spell ...'

I watched Bibi carefully the next day. I hid in the corners of the house without being seen, to see what she would say to Mother. But Bibi didn't say anything. The fact that she could keep a secret thrilled me, and removed some of my fears and anxieties. That noon I lay next to her and spoke more comfortably, 'Bibi ... the spell.'

The less fear I had the more words I could speak. Bibi was calm and wouldn't get excited whenever I said something. She didn't seem unusually happy, and didn't make fun of me. It was as if the fact that I spoke was a very natural thing and had never been an issue. After a month Bibi and I talked to each other without any problem, and this was a special secret between the two of us. Bibi didn't want to show off my speaking, didn't feel like she had to prove something. She didn't want to put me on display, and most importantly, she didn't betray my trust in her.

CHAPTER 39

'Shahaab's totally different when he's with you. You seem to really understand him.'

'Why couldn't you understand him?'

'He's so complicated, I couldn't figure out what to do with him.'

'The only solution is love and kindness, which you don't show him.'

'What a thing to say! All I think and worry about all day is him. You can't imagine how upset I am over him, constantly making sure no one bullies him.'

'What a strange show of love! You only worry about him, but don't enjoy his presence. You show your concern, but not your love. I've never seen you hug and kiss him the way you hug and kiss Shadi.'

'Shadi is a baby, I can't ignore her. Whenever I approach Shahaab he runs away.'

'I didn't say you should ignore Shadi, but you should pay attention to Shahaab too. Ask yourself why he runs away.'

'Believe me, Mother, I've been to so many specialists and read so many books about his condition, but whatever we do is no use.'

'Back in our time, we didn't read as much as you do now, but we lived more comfortably with our kids. Our children had fewer problems and grew up more naturally. The story of love is written on your heart, it's not something you'll find in a book. You don't need to be highly educated in order to read it.'

'I worry so much that I've almost forgotten about love.'

'That's it. That's all you know how to do – worry, complain about your kids and put faults on them. You've talked about it so much that he's come to believe there's something wrong with him.'

'Don't you think there is?'

'No, not at all!'

'You don't think he's retarded?'

'Of course not! He's actually quite smart.'

'I say the same thing to everyone, but honestly, I don't believe it any longer. He does such strange things, making mischief and hurting people who haven't done anything to him, even dangerous things. Sometimes I think he could even kill someone! If he had the strength he would have hurt his father by now.'

'This child doesn't do anything without a reason. You just can't understand his reasons. You treat him abnormally.'

'Because he isn't a normal child!'

'Stop all this rubbish! He's no different from any other child.'

'What do you mean? Normal kids his age will go to school this year, but in his situation, he'll have to go to a special school. I've been to a hundred schools, and none of them will take him.' And with that I burst into tears.

'You have to prove to them he's just like other kids. You have to hurry up and enrol him.'

CHAPTER 40

One afternoon, in the quiet of our room, Bibi asked, 'Don't you want to go to school?'

I confidently answered, 'No, I don't like it!'

'But going to school is fun.'

'I don't want to go. I'll get tired.'

'Tired? All the kids there are your age. You'll learn to read and write. Then you can read books on your own. If you don't learn how to read and write, you won't be able to do anything when you grow up.'

I went deep into thought. None of Bibi's reasons were convincing enough for me to accept the burden of going to school. All the children my age were strangers who scared me. Reading alone wasn't any fun either. The only interesting things in books were the pictures, which you could look at without being able to read. And growing up and finding a job was so far away. The only image I had of growing up was Father's scowling face when he got back from work. He would nag at Mother, and ban us from running around and playing. No! I had no desire to grow up and be like him.

I said, 'I d . . . d . . . don't want to d . . . d . . . do anything when I grow up.'

'Oh, no! What a thing to say! You're a man. When you grow

up you'll get married. If you don't have a job, how are you going to support your wife and children?'

The things Bibi said! Wife and children! I would never get married. I don't like girls. They're all spoiled, like Shadi. The future Bibi talked of was unimaginable to me and didn't motivate me at all.

'No! I won't go. I'll get tired.'

'What do you mean, you'll get tired? People get tired all the time. Then they sleep at night and won't be tired in the morning. You can't keep from doing things just because you'll get tired.'

'Yes, I can.'

Asi said, 'Doesn't Bibi notice that on the weekends Arash's dad is in a better mood, and Arash feels good and isn't tired? Whenever he gets back from school he is so tired and still has to do a lot of homework! He even cries sometimes because he's so tired.'

'My darling, school isn't that hard or tiring, especially the first year. You'll play and have fun most of the time, with very little homework.' Bibi talked about school every day. I wasn't sure why she insisted on my going to school so much. But the things she talked about gradually made school more familiar and bearable to me.

CHAPTER 41

Mother got home frustrated and angry. She threw her scarf in a corner and with tears in her eyes said, 'See, I told you, none of the schools will admit him! They say he has to attend a special school.'

'Why? What did you say about him?'

'Nothing, I just said he couldn't talk.'

'Where's the school? I'll go myself. Dress Shahaab. I'm taking him with me.'

'Where to, Mother? You never even went to enrol us in school, now you want to talk to a bunch of strangers for *him*? What are you going to say anyway? We can't lie to them.'

'It's none of your business. I won't tell a single lie.'

With some incredulity Mother got me dressed. She said, 'I'm coming too.'

'No. I have to go alone. You'll ruin everything if you come along.'

She took my hand and we left the house. I couldn't understand exactly what was happening. I worriedly asked Bibi, 'What's wrong?'

'Let's go to the park first and I'll tell you. I want us to make a plan to make fools of them all. To get even with them so they'll never label you again.'

'Make fools of who?'

'Your father, your mother, your grandmother, your uncle and aunt, and everyone else.'

'But how?'

'Let's go and sit there, and I'll tell you.'

We sat on a bench in a small park near our house. Bibi took a deep breath and said, 'Listen, Shahaab, you're the cleverest kid I know.'

'Me? Really?'

'Yes, you are. You're so clever, you've been able to fool them all.'

'Fool them?'

'Yes! You could talk all these years, but you didn't because you were angry with them. They thought you were dumb and treated you like a retarded child. And you never let them know the truth. This is how you made fun of them.'

'I made fun of them?'

'Yes. Good for you! You're very smart. Only smart people can do things like this.'

'But I can't talk.'

'So how come you're talking to me? Remember last year when you swore in front of them? You could speak then, and you can speak now. You just won't because you're afraid of getting caught! I haven't told anyone that you can talk, and this is how we'll continue to make fun of them.'

I began to think. She was right. I could talk, but only to her. I liked the things she said. Had I really made fun of them? I asked doubtfully, 'How will we make fun of them?'

'They've told everyone that you can't talk. That's why they won't admit you at school. We'll trick them. We'll go to school, answer all their questions, and enrol you. They'll all be amazed and we won't tell them how we did it.'

'But I can't talk! I'm afraid! What if I get tongue-tied?'

'You're talking really well now.'

'Because I'm talking to you. I can only talk to you.'

'Well, talk to me when we're at the school. Pretend you're talking to me and ignore everyone else.'

178

'What if I go mute?'

'It's not important at all. You'll talk if you can and you won't if you can't. Most kids are shy in front of strangers anyway. This isn't anything new for the head and the teachers there. They won't be upset or surprised.'

More than speaking at school, I was afraid of what would happen later at home.

Babi said, 'What if Mother and Arash's father find out? They'll make us talk in front of everyone. Then we'll get tongue-tied and mute again. Everyone will laugh and say we're dumb.'

I got very scared and started to breathe fast.

'So, what do you say? Should we go? Don't worry about anything. I'll answer all their questions. They may just ask your name. Are you ready?'

'N ... n ... n ... no! What if Arash's f ... f ... father finds out?'

Whenever I thought of Arash's father my stuttering would get worse. Bibi started to think. She was silent for a bit then said, 'Why are you so afraid of your father? What has he done to you? He never scolds you, and I haven't seen him punish you. It's not important if he ever tells you off anyway – most parents do that. Our father always told us off and hit us, but we would forget about it the next day and still loved him. We used to scold and sometimes punish our kids too. Your Uncle Mohsen was such a mischievous child. He got smacked quite often. But he always came back into my arms and hugged me. What has your father done that you can't forgive?'

'You loved Uncle Mohsen even if you hit him.'

She looked at me with surprise. I don't know if she understood what I meant or if she instinctively realized she had to respect how I felt at that moment. She said with determination, 'Very well. You're right. Your father mustn't find out that you can speak. Don't worry, I won't let him find out. When we get home, we'll say they realized you're a smart, good boy so they admitted you at school. We'll say the head said it's not important whether you talk or not, it's only important whether you listen. Just imagine how shocked they'll be! They'll look ridiculous! Ready to go?'

I was hesitant, but making fun of them was a convincing reason for going to school. I followed Bibi with some trepidation.

CHAPTER 42

I imagined a million scary scenarios until they finally got home. I hurried towards them with concern and said, 'Where have you been in this heat and your leg in such pain?! You need to rest. Why don't you take better care of yourself?'

'We went to school. Shahaab wanted to see his new school.' She gave Shahaab a wink.

'Mother! Don't say such things in front of this child. I told you, they won't admit him this year. He'll go to speech therapy this year, and maybe they'll enrol him at school next year.'

'What a strange person you are! You need to cure yourself. He's not going to any specialist, and I've already signed him up for school. These are the things you need to do and the stuff you need to get for him.' She handed me a piece of paper. I looked at it in astonishment.

'Mother, what did you do? Did you lie? They'll eventually find out he has a problem. Then they'll expel him from school!'

'This child's only problem is you.'

'What's that supposed to mean?'

'Just what I said! You are this child's problem. They saw Shahaab, tested him and said he's fine, he's better than fine, and they admitted him to school. Do you have a problem with that? Take me upstairs, Shahaab, I'm getting tired here.'

I heard voices inside the room. I slowly opened the door. The glass of lemonade shook in my hand. Shahaab jumped up and down and said, 'I'll write! I'll write!' Bibi laughed out loud. They both went silent as soon as they saw me. I placed the glass of lemonade on the desk. My eyes filled with tears. I opened my arms and went towards Shahaab, but he slipped from under them, went out of the room and ran downstairs. I sat on the bed.

'Why didn't you tell me anything? Was I a stranger? I've been praying for him to talk for all these years!' And I began to cry.

'Dearest, you need to understand, I couldn't say anything. I promised him. If I betrayed him he wouldn't trust anyone ever again.'

'Why is he like this? Why did he make such a big deal of it? All the other children speak so easily and don't make an issue of it.'

'He made a big deal of it because you did.'

'Of course we did. At first they said he couldn't talk because he had a Turkish-speaking nanny, which confused him. Later they said it was because of Shadi, that he needed more time now that there was a new baby in the house. But then when he still couldn't talk, we were convinced he must have a mental problem of some sort.'

'But he didn't have any problems. You just made such a big deal of it, doing all sorts of strange things, so that he became afraid and didn't dare to speak.'

'He was even afraid of *me*? I was always his defender and he knows how much I love him. Why didn't he talk to me?'

'No! He doesn't know how much you love him. How can he? You need to show your love. Do you think shedding a few tears and showing you're sad is the same as showing your love? Whenever you want to show affection you just sigh and say, "Your sorrow will be the death of me." Your home is so depressing! What's wrong with you, why are you always frowning? You're my child and I always used to sing and dance over everything. Everyone always talked so much at our home that you could never tell who was saying what.'

'Mother, my problem is that I went from that rowdy, lively home to one where everyone is so serious and quiet. If I don't talk, Nasser can stay quiet for an entire week and not say a word. I've lost all my enjoyment of life.'

'Why are you such a coward? I expected more from you. You should talk even if he doesn't. Make him answer you.'

'How much can I say on my own? It's as if nothing I say is interesting to him. I've become passive too. How long can you go on having a conversation with a statue? I won't lower myself more than this.'

'Lower yourself? What a thing to say. Are you demeaning yourself when you talk to someone this close to you?'

'It's not as if I can force him to talk. Plus, he gets angry when I get on his case, so I've given up. The less we rub each other up the wrong way the better. I consistently try to keep things calm and quiet so it doesn't have a negative effect on the kids.'

'Even if you argued it would be better than the silence that rules your house now. It's as if you're on bad terms, or don't like each other at all. Tell me, do you love your husband? You two got married because you loved each other. Even though we didn't care much for his grumpy, vain mother, and preferred to have you near us, your father and I agreed because we thought you were in love. So what happened to you two?'

'I don't know! The pressures of life haven't left any room for love.'

'Rubbish! The harder life is, the more one needs a mate to confide in.'

'You don't understand, Mother. Sometimes keeping quiet is better than talking. Sometimes we say things to each other that are hurtful – it makes us argue. Sometimes we say things we shouldn't.'

'Was it always this way or is this something new?'

'To tell you the truth I think it began with Shahaab. Nasser acts as if he's been insulted – he feels like a failure and sort of holds me responsible. He doesn't say anything, but that's what I think.'

183

'What in the world? I know men are proud and can't accept that their offspring may not be perfect, but I never imagined an educated man would think that way!'

'Well, he does, but he doesn't come right out and say it. Remember Kal-Abbass? Remember when his son was born with six fingers, he made a fuss, denying it was his child and divorced his wife right there and then? It's the same thing.'

'And what about you? You're not like Kal-Abbass's wife, waiting for him to divorce you!'

'Oh, Mother, I'm so tired and depressed that I've lost all my self-confidence. Once I could stand up to everyone, but now I can't any more. It's as if I've accepted that I'm to blame. Nasser doesn't say anything; I don't want you to think he accuses me of anything. From a scientific, medical point of view he knows it's not my fault. But he's not proud of the child and can't bring himself to say it's his son.'

'So that's why the child calls him "Arash's father".'

'Are you serious? He calls him "Arash's father"?'

'Shahaab is smarter than you and me. He records everything like a camera and stores it in his brain. I don't think he'll ever forgive his father's behaviour.'

'He really says "Arash's father"?'

'Yes!'

'He says it? He expresses his feelings to you? He says all these things?'

'You heard him. He talks, and he talks well.'

'How did he learn so fast?'

'He didn't learn so fast. He's been able to talk for several years now. He talks in his head, with his imaginary friends, with people he can trust.'

'So why won't he speak to us?'

'You should ask yourselves that question. He's afraid of you. And you have to act accordingly if you don't want him to become mute again. You can't announce it all over the place. You can't make a show out of it. You can't turn him into a clown, forcing him to perform in front of the crowd. The things you did the first time around actually frighten me. Even I get flustered and tongue-tied in front of your husband's rude family, who don't have an ounce of kindness between them.'

'Did he tell you these things himself?'

'Yes, some of it. And I guessed the rest.'

CHAPTER 43

Bibi lay down on a blanket in the corner of the room and laughed, 'Did you see how surprised she was? She couldn't believe it!'

'She was upset!'

'No, darling, she was just surprised. When she finally believes it, she'll be so happy. And you said your name very well at school today.'

'Really? Did they all hear me?'

'Of course, sweetheart!'

'Will I have to talk to everyone at school? What if I go mute? Everyone will laugh.'

'You won't go mute. It didn't happen today, did it? All the other kids are like you too. It's not important if they laugh, you can laugh along with them. You're going to learn how to read and write, and then you can write down whatever you want to say. You can talk when you want to, and write down what you want to say when you don't feel like talking.'

Write! Yes, I could write things instead of saying them. She was right! How cool! I'd suddenly discovered an alternative for talking, which was still so difficult for me to do. What an amazing discovery! This was definitely a convincing reason for going to school. I yelled, 'You're right, Bibi. I'll write! I'll write!'

Mother walked in right at that moment and realized I could speak.

Bibi stayed with us for two weeks after school started. When she was sure that I didn't have any problems and could go to school like other children, she packed her bags and went home. I couldn't leave her embrace when we were saying goodbye. She was the only one who understood and loved me just the way I was. On the way back from the station I couldn't stop crying. Father said in a low voice, 'I didn't realize this child could be so emotional and attached to someone else.'

Mother gestured towards me and hushed him. Ever since they'd realized I could speak, they wouldn't say everything in front of me.

Everyone knew I could speak now, but according to Bibi's rules, which Mother followed diligently, they didn't make a fuss out of it and behaved carefully around me. No one asked me any questions, but they tried indirectly to hear my voice. Asi, Babi and I laughed so much over this.

Asi said, 'They think we don't know what they're waiting for. They look away, pretending they aren't paying any attention, but they're all ears!'

Babi said, 'As soon as we open our mouths everyone goes silent, they even stop breathing!'

But it wasn't important any longer. The issue of speaking lost its significance, and I wasn't afraid now. I didn't care if others heard me when I spoke. I stuttered less and less. Speaking to Mother and Shadi at home was the easiest. The others eventually heard my voice and became convinced I could speak, and the issue of my speech was never brought up again in family discussions. Father was the only one who could never talk to me and didn't hear my voice. I was extremely careful to keep my distance from him. We passed by each other like a couple of strangers. I even spoke with Grandmother and Uncle, but was unwilling to answer a simple 'yes' or 'no' to his questions. He wouldn't take any steps forwards, and I wasn't willing to admit defeat and didn't have any intention of making him happy.

Despite my initial fears I began to enjoy school. I had a strong motivation for going. I wanted to learn to write as soon as possible, in case I lost the power of speech again. It was as if speaking was still a nightmare in the back of my mind. I had also promised to write letters to Bibi. I felt this was the only way I could show my gratitude to her, to do something to reward her for all the affection and kindness she'd shown me.

Words were not just a series of letters to me. They each represented their own world. Over my years of speechlessness, I'd struggled with each word. I knew the weight and colour of each one and felt its volume. How could I express all the qualities of a word just by writing it? This is why writing in a single colour was difficult for me. I needed all my coloured pencils in order to do homework. I had to write 'blood' with a red pencil, and black was a more appropriate colour for 'death'. I used green for 'love' and grey for 'sadness'. In my eyes 'Father' was always an unpleasant brown and 'Mother' was a dull yellow, like the sun subdued by dark clouds. For a long time my biggest challenge was using white for 'kindness', which was hard to do on a white piece of paper. I discovered the solution after several attempts. I found out that if I drew the outline of the word with black and left it white on the inside, it would still be legible. I carefully wrote each word in a beautiful script using the correct colours. My insensitive teacher considered my colourful homework a sign of mischief and called them drawings. Finally, by complaining to my mother, she made me use only a black pencil in spelling tests because I couldn't keep up with the rest of the class.

That numbers were different colours was an obvious thing to me, and I assumed this was how everyone saw them. How could people not see the beautiful greenish hue of the number eight, or that seven is the colour of pistachios? But I was always a bit doubtful about the blue of the number three because it changed from time to time. One day as I was doing homework on the kitchen table while Mother was preparing food I asked her, 'Is three a dark blue or a light blue?'

Mother turned around and said, 'What?'

'I asked if three was a dark blue or a light blue? Sometimes it's dark, especially in thirteen.'

I could see the confusion in Mother's eyes. After a while she said, 'What are you talking about? Stop this nonsense at once! People are just beginning to realize you're normal, but if they hear you talk like this they'll think you've gone mad again.'

'But what did I say?'

'That three is blue! Numbers don't have colours! Don't repeat it ever again, okay?'

I looked at her in amazement. As if he'd discovered something important, Babi said, 'She doesn't see the colour of numbers?'

Asi said, 'Maybe no one does.'

'Then why can we see them?'

'Because we're stupid and crazy.'

'I'm glad we are, otherwise we'd have a colourless world just like them!'

From then on, I only used a black pencil to write numbers, even though they were still colourful in my eyes.

CHAPTER 44

I felt vindicated when Shahaab received his school report. I showed it to Grandmother, his uncle and essentially the rest of the world. Whenever I wanted to take revenge on them I'd say, 'I think he's even smarter than Arash!'

I felt stronger after this victory, and our home had a more pleasant atmosphere. Nasser's bruised pride also began to heal with Shahaab's straight As. But Shahaab still wouldn't say a single word to his father. I couldn't tell if Nasser was angry about this or sad. In any case, his pride wouldn't allow him to take the first step in repairing their relationship. It was as if he was embarrassed by this seven-year-old child. The only way for maintaining his pride was to give Shahaab the cold shoulder, waiting for him to take a step forwards. He bought him a bigger bike as an award for his report. Shahaab was very excited when he saw the bike, but he tried not to show it in front of his father. I took advantage of the situation and said, 'Shahaab, don't you want to thank your father? See how much he loves you? He's bought you another bike!'

He very calmly replied, 'He didn't buy it for me. He bought it for my school report.'

'What's that supposed to mean? It's your report – you got good grades so he's bought you a prize.'

'He bought it for my grades.'

'I don't understand what you're saying. You have to thank him. You can't ride the bike until you thank him.'

I was sure the gift Nasser had bought him had affected Shahaab and made him more flexible. It wasn't easy for him to disregard the bike. He accepted that he had to thank Nasser, even though he pretended I was dragging him there. He hung his head, stood in front of Nasser and in the lowest possible voice said, 'Thanks!'

I pushed him towards Nasser and said, 'No, just a plain thanks won't do. You have to kiss him too.'

He looked at Nasser from the corner of his eye and slowly took a step forwards. Nasser didn't budge. He sat there cool and indifferent, pretending to read the paper. It was as if saying thank you and kissing him were Shahaab's obvious duties, and didn't make any difference to Nasser. Shahaab's hand shook in mine and his lips quivered. The positive feelings he had developed when he had seen the bike evaporated with his father's coolness and victorious pose. Shahaab pulled his hand away, trying to run off. I picked him up and held his face next to Nasser's cheek. He turned his face away, struggled and slid out of my arms, and ran up the stairs.

Nasser looked on with a reproving glance and said, 'There you are! This is how your son thanks me! He's so stubborn.'

I replied venomously, 'Just like yourself! Stubborn and vindictive!'

CHAPTER 45

My second-year teacher noticed my handwriting early on. She always complimented me on it and sometimes would ask with surprise, 'Did you write this yourself?'

I would nod my head with pride and, without a word, would repeat it in front of her. She encouraged me, and I tried to write better and better. One day she said, 'Shahaab, dear, ask your father to come to school tomorrow. I need to ask him something.'

I looked at her, annoyed. What does she want with my father? I said, 'He doesn't want to!'

'What do you mean? He has to come. I need to speak to him about how well you're doing.'

'My mother will come instead.'

'But I would rather talk to your father. I need to ask his permission for something.'

'No.'

The teacher looked at me curiously and said, 'Why not? Don't you want your father to come to see your work and be pleased?'

'No!'

'But why? He's such a good father. He drops you off at school every morning.'

'I just don't want to.'

'How come? Isn't he your father?'

'No!'

'What?! So who was it who said "Hi" to me this morning?'

'Arash's father.'

'Arash? Your brother in middle school?'

'Yes!'

I didn't feel like talking any more. I took my biscuits and went outside. The teacher was still looking at me curiously as I went out of the door.

As usual I was sitting in the playground looking at other children playing. I really wanted to join in but something inside kept me back. I still felt like I was different from them. I couldn't forget that all the other kids were clever and I was stupid. I was eating my biscuits when I noticed the third-year teacher, along with my own teacher and the deputy head Mrs Rasouli, looking at me from a terrace overlooking the grounds. They kept pointing at me and chatting. A few of the teachers were also looking through the office window. I felt slightly afraid and tried to hide among the other kids.

CHAPTER 46

Mother started going to work again. We all got into Father's car in the mornings. Firstly, we would drop Shadi off at the child-care centre. Mother would get off at the bus stop and take the bus to work. Then we would drop Arash off, and I would be the last person to be dropped off. One day, Mother didn't get out at the bus stop. I thought she must be going somewhere else and paid no attention to it. Father was upset about something too, but this was nothing new. After Arash got out, he finally looked at Mother and said, 'Ask him what he's done. Why are they so insistent for us to go to his school? I have a ton of things to do and had to cancel a meeting today!'

'Hush! You don't need to make such a fuss. Nothing will happen if you're half an hour late.'

'Couldn't you go by yourself?'

'Apparently they need to meet you. I told them you were busy and I could go instead, but the head insisted they would either meet the both of us, or you alone.'

I finally realized they were coming to my school and became very anxious.

The three of us stood in the head's office like guilty school kids. I felt that Mother and Arash's father were as afraid as I was. They had rung the bell and the children were going to class in rows. The teachers had crowded into the office. The head said with a kind smile, 'Mr and Mrs Mokhtari, please, take a seat.' The teachers all turned silent, staring at my parents. I stood next to Mother and pressed myself against her. The fifth-year teacher greeted Father and asked after Arash.

Father calmed down as soon as he heard Arash's name. His eyes lit up and he said, 'He's very well, a straight-A student as usual.'

'He'll be successful when he grows up.'

The teachers headed to class one by one. The office was quieter now. Mrs Rasouli, the deputy head, pretended to look through some folders in a corner, but she was clearly more interested in us. The head tried to seem friendly and said, 'Mr Mokhtari, I heard you were a member of the PTA until two years ago. Unfortunately I wasn't at this school back then, so wasn't fortunate enough to make your acquaintance. But Mr Atayi, the administrative assistant, and Mrs Sadeghi, the fifth-year teacher, mentioned all you did for the school and your attentiveness towards Arash's education. No wonder he was always at the top of his class.'

I felt Dad grow taller. He said with pride, 'Mr Atayi and Mrs Sadeghi are very kind. Arash is a very smart boy. There may be very few kids like him. He's at the top of his class in middle school too. Everyone thinks he should attend a special school for advanced students. What's your opinion on this?'

'Well, I don't agree with advanced schools that much, but that's an entirely different discussion. I wanted to talk to you about Shahaab today.'

Father frowned once again and said, 'What's the trouble this time?'

'Does he often get into trouble?'

I peeked from behind the chair. The head noticed me and said, 'Shahaab, go to class please.'

I left the office worried and upset.

Asi said, 'I wish we'd hidden behind the chair till the end, so he wouldn't have seen us.'

CHAPTER 47

My heart sank as soon as the head said he wanted to talk to us about Shahaab. When Nasser and he started discussing whether my son was any trouble, I jumped in and said, 'But I'm in touch with his teachers all the time! They say he's a good boy and no one has ever complained about him.'

'Yes, he's a very good boy, but a bit shy. He hardly interacts with other children.'

'Yes, I know. He's always been this way. Actually he's improved quite a lot.'

'Really? Of course his shyness is understandable given his situation at home.'

Nasser sadly asked, 'What situation? He's not lacking for anything at home. We've spent our lives taking care of him. What more should we do? Do you know how many doctors we took him to for his lack of speech?'

'I'm not speaking of material comforts. What I meant was being humane and affectionate.'

Nasser said, 'Do you mean to say we haven't treated him humanely? That we haven't attended to him enough? His mother has spoilt him so much that no one in the family, including me, dares to criticize him for the slightest thing!'

'Don't be so angry – there is no need to become defensive, Mr

Mokhtari. I have a lot of respect for you, but I wish you paid a bit more attention to his emotional well-being. I know you try to, but maybe sometimes unconsciously you favour your own children over him. Children are very sensitive and notice things we wouldn't. I just thought it was my duty to inform you of this situation.'

Nasser and I both looked at the head, dumbfounded.

Nasser said, 'Excuse me, but I don't understand a word you're saying. Did you say I favour my own children over him? What's that supposed to mean?'

'I apologize. I realize this must be a sensitive issue and you probably don't like talking about it, but here at the school, we must know everything about the children in order to be able to help them better.'

'Know what?'

'Shahaab knows very well that he isn't your child.'

Nasser turned red. He looked at the head in confusion.

I had a hunch about what had happened and said, 'Has he said something?'

'Yes.'

Nasser pursed his lips, turned to me and said, 'What are they talking about?'

'I don't know exactly. I can guess, but I didn't think Shahaab would take it as far as talking to other people about it.'

'Take what as far? Tell me what's going on here!'

But I still wasn't sure. I turned to the head and asked, 'Please repeat everything. How did you come to this conclusion?'

'He told his teacher.'

Nasser was getting angrier and angrier. He said in a loud voice, 'What are you saying, sir?'

In order to make him quieten down I said, 'Sir, this man is my husband and the father of my three children, Arash, Shahaab, and Shadi. We don't have an unusual family situation here. It's not right for you to question us over something a kid says. Why didn't you ask me yourself?'

The head mumbled, 'We didn't believe it either.' He was

lying. 'That's why we asked you to come here. The child claims that your husband is Arash's father and not his. We thought we should discuss the issue with you. It is important that you're aware of his feelings towards his parents and what he thinks about them. I will call his teacher in so she can explain everything.'

The deputy head, who was sitting on the other side of the room, no longer even pretended to be working. I felt we'd been called here to satisfy their curiosity more than anything else. Nasser was going crazy, and said, 'He says I'm not his father?'

'Unfortunately, yes.'

The door opened and the teacher walked in. Without greeting her I said abruptly, 'Mrs Kamali, please tell us exactly what Shahaab said to you.'

She looked guilty and flustered, and said, 'I wanted to meet you to see if you would agree to buy a present for Shahaab. You know, the school doesn't have enough of a budget for these sorts of things. Parents usually buy the gifts and we hand them to the students during the morning register. I also wanted to ask your permission to sign him up for a special class. Shahaab has beautiful handwriting and I wanted to encourage him and have him train more. That's all! I told him to ask his father to come to school and he said no. I insisted, and he said his mother would come instead. I was surprised because I remembered his father was very involved in school meetings when your elder son attended here. That's why I wanted to meet him. I asked about his father again, and he said he didn't have one. I said who's the person who drops you off at school, and he said "That's Arash's father"!'

Nasser seemed to grow smaller with each word. He was hunched over in his chair. He angrily got up and said, 'Get up! Let's get out of here. I can't stand it any longer!' And he left the office.

I got up, picked up my handbag, turned to his teacher and the head, and said, 'I'll discuss this with you later.' And followed Nasser outside.

Nasser felt terrible. He couldn't control himself. He hurried into the car and said, 'Did you know all this? Did he tell you too?'

'No, not me. But he'd told Bibi. Now that I think about it, I can't recall him ever calling you "Father".'

'What have you lot done to turn him so much against me?'

'What have we done? Why don't you examine yourself and see what *you've* done that has made him unable to see you as his father?'

'What have I done? Actually what haven't I done for him? I was so worried about him all these years. I spent so much money on him. I almost worked myself to death, saving enough money to take him abroad to be cured. And this is how he repays me. He does these things on purpose. He wants to humiliate me. He didn't say a word and acted mute all that time. We tried everything to get him to talk, saw all sorts of specialists, but then realized he was just being stubborn! And now that he talks, this is the kind of rubbish he says! "You're not my father." To hell with him! I never wanted the bastard anyway. "My father is someone else." Probably the man who found him that other time. Remember how he would hug him just to annoy me? I wished he would speak to me just once, call me "Father" just once.' His voice broke and he turned his face away so I wouldn't see his tears.

'Nasser, he's just a boy.'

'Yes, but he's my greatest enemy. No one can get on my nerves like he can.'

'You have to try to understand him. You have to be patient with him. You have to try to find out why he thinks this way. Maybe you haven't shown him enough affection. Don't you think you were a bit inattentive towards him?'

'No! Not at all! Our entire life was taken over by this child. We never had any problems with Arash or Shadi. All our thoughts and concerns have focused on him.'

'It's not such a big deal. He's a kid and he said something silly.'

'How can I not let it upset me? There are many kids who don't have their fathers around, and they still claim them as fathers. Yet here I am, present in his life, working day and night to take care of him, to feed and clothe him, and he goes and says he doesn't have a father! That I'm not his father! Can you imagine how that feels?' And he started to cry again.

CHAPTER 48

That afternoon, as I was having a snack in the kitchen, Mother said, 'Your father is very upset.' I shrugged my shoulders. 'Do you know why he's so sad?' I turned around, uninterested. 'Because of the things you've said. You've really hurt him.'

I looked at her in surprise, 'Me!'

'Yes, you.'

I knew it had something to do with school. I thought he was upset because I'd sworn at one of the kids at school. Distractedly I said, 'It's okay. He's always upset with me. All the other children swear too.'

'This has nothing to do with swearing. He's sad because you told your teacher he wasn't your father.'

'Is that all? Well, he's not.'

'What do you mean? After all he's done for you, clothing and feeding you, paying for school, the doctors and a million other things! He's always worried about you, and then you go and embarrass him, saying he's not your father?'

'I always embarrass him.'

'Why do you hate him so much?'

'He's Arash's father because Arash is a good boy. But I'm a bad boy, and I'm dumb. If I *were* his kid he'd always be embarrassed. I can't help it.'

'What a thing to say! You're not dumb at all. In fact you're quite clever.'

'No I'm not. I'm only *your* son.'

'No. You're both his and mine.'

'Don't you know that good kids belong to fathers and bad kids belong to mothers?'

'Where do you get these ideas? Who said you're bad? You're a very good boy and it would be anyone's dream to have a son just like you.'

'Like me?'

'Yes, you! Your father is very hurt that you said you're not his child.'

'You're lying. Arash's father is upset because I've embarrassed him.'

'No, sweetheart. He wants to be your father too. If he's not your father, then who is? You can't be without a father. Every child needs a father.'

'No. Nader doesn't have a father.'

'Who's Nader?'

'He lives in the house at the end of the alley.'

'He used to have a father, but he passed away.'

'What does passing away mean?'

'It means he's dead.'

'Maybe mine's dead too.'

'God forbid! Your father is very healthy. You have to love him. He works all day for you children. Where would we get money if he weren't around? How would we buy clothes and food? We would have to live on the streets and we would die of hunger. You should be grateful that you have a father.'

I listened to her with surprise. To me there was no connection between loving my father and dying of hunger. She made up such strange things! I was silent for a while and then said, 'Don't worry. Nader doesn't have a father, but he lives in a house and hasn't died of hunger either.'

CHAPTER 49

A few days later I went back to Shahaab's school and talked to the head and his teacher. The misunderstanding was resolved and the head was happy to learn that I only had one husband. Mrs Kamali apologized and said, 'I didn't want things to get out of hand like this, but as soon as I mentioned Arash and Shahaab Mokhtari were stepbrothers, all the teachers became so interested in it. Some thought you'd been married twice, and others claimed you had been married three times. But everyone wanted to find out why you'd returned to your first husband. It's strange that none of us thought the child might be lying!'

'We'd better drop it altogether. This has really affected my husband.'

'We're so sorry.'

'It's okay. I'm here now to see what you wanted from the start.'

'As I mentioned befor, Shahaab has a real talent in writing and drawing. I have taught the second year for twenty years and have never had a student with such a beautiful hand. My husband is a calligrapher. I showed him some of Shahaab's handwriting and he said it was fascinating because his style is so highly developed. He couldn't believe it was the work of a second-year pupil. He said he'd like to train him.'

I retold the story over supper. Arash said, 'My handwriting

was good too. Remember I used to do the text for all the school posters?'

'Yes. Your fifth-year teacher was there and she remembered your writing. But Mrs Kamali said they've had many kids with beautiful handwriting, but Shahaab is exceptional.'

Shahaab pretended to be busy eating, and tried to hide his joy. He peeked at Nasser from the corner of his eye, but Nasser was quiet and didn't react.

I said, 'So, Nasser, what do you say? Mrs Kamali said he could go to her husband's calligraphy class twice a week if you allow it. What do you think we should do? Should we sign him up for lessons?'

'I don't know. After all, I'm not his father!'

We all turned quiet. Shahaab stared at his plate for a while, then quietly put his spoon down, left the kitchen and went upstairs.

I followed him up and sat on his bed next to him.

'Shahaab, stop playing these games. If you want to take lessons and if you like calligraphy, you need to ask your father to sign you up.'

He turned around and pretended to go to sleep.

'I guess you don't really want to go. I'll tell your teacher that your father wanted to sign you up for lessons, but that you didn't want to go.' I got up to leave.

From underneath the covers Shahaab said, 'Sign me up yourself.'

'Me? Why not him?'

'You do it. I don't want him to come to school.'

'He's your father. If he doesn't give his permission, and if he doesn't pay for the lessons, I can't do it. Fathers have to give their permission for everything their children want to do.'

'If Bibi were here, she'd sign me up herself.'

I hesitated. I didn't want him to think I was weaker and more helpless than Bibi. But I also didn't want to undermine the importance of his father. I said, 'Okay. I'll ask your father for permission. If he says yes and agrees to pay for the classes, I'll sign you up myself.'

CHAPTER 50

My school years slowly went by. I was a good pupil. I wasn't at the top of my class and didn't try to be. There were always some in the class that had to be top students to please their parents, and they fought hard for that achievement. I wasn't stupid enough to put myself through such hardship for such a silly goal. Luckily, no one expected it from me either. That had been poor Arash's responsibility from the start, and to achieve it, he had to go to many classes, never having any time for himself. I only went to calligraphy, and was very excited on the day of my class.

I was always surprised at how fast the hour of my lesson went. I had time to read other things, to think and even to play, and I was often astonished to find that Arash, despite being a genius, didn't know some of the things I knew. He didn't know how to play certain games, even didn't know some of the slang kids used. To be first in your class you had to constantly read schoolbooks and worry about others getting better marks. And when they did, you would burn with jealousy, have nightmares or get ill, like Arash did that year because he'd come second in his class.

As I wasn't considered dumb any more, Arash had it slightly better than usual because Father wasn't as determined to prove his genius. But now, my brother couldn't let go of that. He insisted on being first; it was as if he wasn't good enough if he didn't come top in his class. He always had to show how smart he was. He had to pretend he knew more than anyone else, but he was afraid, because he realized he didn't. I felt sorry for him. The poor boy wasn't allowed to make any mistakes. Since he'd started senior school, he now had an additional nightmare in his life: university entrance exams. He constantly had stomach-aches from stress. He always kept his hand on his stomach, had to abstain from certain foods and walked bent over like an old man. He didn't even have any real friends. If his best friend got a better mark than him, he would become his greatest enemy. He was usually lonely, and that's what drew him to books. I knew he didn't even like books now, but it seemed as if he was missing something without them; something important like an arm or a leg. Now *he* was the source of Mother's worries.

She once said to Father, 'This child is sick with stress. I'm afraid he'll give everything up one of these days.'

'It'll get better once he enters the university.'

'What if he doesn't get in? What then?'

'He will. What's important is that he falls within the first percentile. He has to get into Tehran University's medical school.'

'If you want to know the truth, sometimes when I see how lonely, worried and empty of fun his life is, I wish he'd rebel against everything, even though I realize how dangerous that might be. Sometimes I wish he'd give it all up and learn to enjoy his life and his youth. Believe me, he's more at risk than either Shahaab or Shadi.'

Mother was right. Arash crumbled like a wall when he didn't get accepted into medical school. He had to be hospitalized for depression and extreme mental anxiety. He grew to hate text-books. He was under a doctor's care for three years until he became a normal person again. He came to realize that he hadn't liked medicine to start with, and had wanted to study literature instead.

I was free of this misery. And Shadi was even better off than me. It was as if she had never experienced sadness. She knew that everyone loved her just the way she was. She didn't care or worry about being the best and was never jealous. No one expected anything but love and kindness from her and she didn't expect anything else either. She wasn't shy like I was, and talked and laughed easily with other people. She had many friends. In effect, she was a healthy, happy child and had such strong self-confidence that nothing could shake her good humour or sense of security.

Mother changed once she started working again. It was as though she felt more important and was no longer a pushover like she'd been when I was dumb. She seemed happier and nagged less, even though she had more to do and less time to attend to the house. She didn't have time now to worry about what the family said, so no one could get on her nerves. She had always been ready to take offence at the slightest remark, but now she gradually became less sensitive. She was friendly towards Grandmother and the others, and very soon forgot everything they said. She would say, 'They have sharp tongues but kind hearts. They just don't know how to show their kindness.'

Fataneh and Uncle Hossein's family were dealing with their own problems. To keep Fereshteh from falling in love again, which might have led to another disaster, they wed her to a thirty-something-year-old when she was only seventeen. The groom apparently met all the prerequisites. He was educated, wealthy, good-looking, and owned a house, a car and the necessary accoutrements. Fereshteh got a significant *mahriyeh** and had a lavish wedding; unlike any we'd had in the family before. Fataneh was convinced her daughter's future was bright. Fereshteh moved into her new house. She had everything she could hope for, but still dreamed of Ramin at night. No one heard her loud, joyful laugh again. She became a shopaholic, constantly buying clothes, jewellery and appliances, but she soon lost her interest in money and shopping, and began taking antidepressants. She still talked to me

---

* A dowry in the form of money or property made to the bride from the groom, at the time of marriage.

every once in a while, but she spoke so cautiously that I couldn't understand half the things she said. I think she doesn't know what's wrong with herself either.

Khosrow failed school for two years in a row and fell behind Arash. The most important things in his life were the brands he wore. He bought expensive shoes and fashionable clothes, and didn't care whether or not his father could afford to pay for his extravagances. Fataneh always had his back though. She used all sorts of ways to find money to buy him the things he wanted. Khosrow never appreciated her and always expected more, quickly growing bored with the things he had. He was also very competitive with his friends and was willing to do dangerous things to surpass them. He was bold and ready to try anything. He would take his father's car without permission and drive his friends around Tehran's busy streets, while talking to his girlfriends on the mobile phone his mother had bought him with borrowed money. His gel-styled spiky hair was a thorn in my uncle's side. One day, Uncle Hossein told Father, 'Every time I look at him it's as if someone's calling me a four-letter word! He always wants something or other, and is constantly getting into trouble. I'm really worried about his future, but I think he's a lost cause. Nothing can be done for him now.'

Father was the most important person in our household, but he was like a shadow we felt on us only when he was actually present. He saw himself as a money-making machine, and we'd come to view him the same way, expecting nothing more than his pay cheque. He was always tired, but was less angry than before. His relationship with Mother had improved, and they behaved almost like two equals. When I was still in junior school, Mother used to speak of his sacrifices to make me love him, but I resisted and tried to have as little contact with him as possible. I answered his questions with the shortest possible words, and tried not to ask him for anything. I even got my pocket money from Mother. It seemed to me he was waiting for me to fail in my self-devised war with him, but I was still hurt and couldn't forget my childhood sense of unwantedness.

CHAPTER 51

Shahaab took the first prize in his writing class every year. His handiwork became more and more beautiful. Words still seemed magical to him. The years of not being able to speak had given such weight to words, infusing their meanings with colours and scents in his mind, which were all expressed in the pieces he made. His teacher excitedly said, 'He writes the souls of words. What he does is not simple calligraphy any more, it is a work of art filled with meaning. I think even an illiterate person can understand what he writes.'

Shahaab really liked his teacher and got along with him. He liked spending his free time there. Nasser wasn't pleased at all and came up with different excuses to keep him from going. Shahaab would get upset and complain to me. I was afraid of another outburst between them and tried to justify his father's decisions.

'You know, Shahaab, your father's jealous. Any man who gets close to you seems like a competitor to him. When he sees how close you are to your teacher he goes green with jealousy.'

He looked at me with surprise and said, 'How odd. "Green with jealousy."' And he went deep into thought.

He had just started his fifth year when his teacher arranged to have one of his pieces displayed at a professional calligraphy exhibition. On the last day of the exhibition there was to be a ceremony where they would award the artists. I was very excited and sent invitations to all the family. Everyone came: Hossein, Fataneh, Khosrow, Shahin, Fereshteh and her husband. When it was Shahaab's turn, his teacher praised his work and his creativity and said they were sending his work to be exhibited in Hungary. Shadi and I were beaming with happiness. Nasser tried to act serious and respectable but he couldn't hide his glowing pride.

Shahaab was invited to receive a prize. I could tell how embarrassed he was. He turned red and walked on to the stage with heavy steps. His teacher bent down, kissed his cheek and handed him a trophy. Everyone applauded. The teacher finally said, 'Shahaab Mokhtari, our dear young artist, would you like to say anything?'

Shahaab shook his head. His teacher continued, 'Then I'll ask your father to kindly come on stage and say a few words about you.'

Nasser shifted uncomfortably in his chair. I became agitated and said, 'Nasser, they're waiting for you.' He took a look around, got up and walked to the stage. His steps seemed shaky.

CHAPTER 52

My teacher said in a formal tone, 'Mr Mokhtari, I congratulate you for having a son like Shahaab. We also consider you prize-worthy, for being such an aware parent, and discovering and developing your son's unusual talent at such an early age. Ladies and gentlemen, this is a very serious issue. There are many talented children that never get the chance to develop because their parents don't have the required awareness. I sincerely hope that other parents follow Mr Mokhtari's example and pay more attention to their children's capabilities.'

I gave a sarcastic grin and lowered my head. My father stepped forwards. Speaking into the microphone made his voice unfamiliar, but the fact that he sounded choked up had nothing to do with the microphone. I looked up, surprised. He looked pale and his lips were trembling. After a long pause he said, 'Having a son like Shahaab is every parent's dream. He has achieved everything on his own. I haven't done anything for him. He deserves more than I've ever given him. I hope he can forgive me.' I was in shock, looking at him in disbelief. 'The only thing I can say is that I love you more than anything else in the world and am extremely proud of you.' He opened his arms and came towards me. My eyes were filled with tears and I couldn't see him clearly. I went to him. He hugged me hard and gave me a kiss on the head.

This scene was photographed and my mother enlarged the photo as if it were a peace agreement following a heart-rending war at home. The framed picture covered half our wall. It was as if she wanted to replace my unhappy childhood memories with this one picture. It eventually became a symbol of my past, hiding my memories behind it.

In the following days some of the ice between us melted. We were both shy and unable to express our feelings, yet we tried to give each other kind glances. But it was too late to learn the art of love, and we needed a long time to make up for lost opportunities. I wasn't sure if that was even possible.

I needed to forget many things in order to love my father the way he deserved. So I began to erase my childhood memories. I still didn't trust him but didn't know why, which made me feel guilty. I felt as if I were an ungrateful child who didn't love my father as much as I should.

The years went by and I successfully completed senior school. Now I am a second-year art student, but I still suffer from a lack of self-confidence and can't easily interact with others. Whenever I decide to say something in a group or express an opinion, my heart starts to beat wildly, making me change my mind about speaking, or else I speak in such a quivering voice that people can barely understand me. Deep inside, I still consider myself stupid. I am never sure of myself or the things I do, and this sense of doubt is apparent in my artwork as well. Mother still worries about me and tries to create situations where I'll meet people my own age. Today she's thrown a large party for my twentieth birthday.

My body felt stiff. I got up from the small platform on the rooftop. I shook the dust off my trousers and peeked over the neighbour's wall. Their tree-filled garden still looked beautiful from above. I could see a nest between some branches. I stretched my hand towards it when I was suddenly startled by a voice. I turned around. Shadi was standing in front of me, beautiful and smiling as always. She pretended to be angry and said,

'So here you are! We've been looking for you for hours! Mother's been holed up in her room and you've been hiding up here like a child! All the guests are waiting for you. What are you doing here?'

'Reviewing the past twenty years.'

'How interesting. Mother said the same thing.'

The living room was filled with people. I joined them. Kourosh, my good-natured, rowdy classmate, pointed to the framed photograph on the wall and said, 'Hey, guys! Come and see this picture. Look at Shahaab. He looks so cute! How long ago was this?'

'I was in the fifth year.'

'Who's the man hugging you like that?'

I stared at the picture and quietly said, 'Him? He's Arash's father!'